DESIRE AT ROOSEVELT RANCH

ROOSEVELT RANCH BOOK 5

ELISE FABER

ACKNOWLEDGMENTS

Thank you my dear readers for following this series from beginning to end! I'm sad that the stories of Darlington and Roosevelt Ranch are coming to a conclusion, but so excited for the new series and projects I'm working on in the meantime. Sign up for my newsletter (http://eepurl.com/bdnmEj) to be kept apprised of all the new and exciting things coming your way.

The Roosevelt Ranch books have been close to my heart for many years now and I hope you've enjoyed the stories of second chances, of mistakes, and of finding your way in the end.

A special thanks to all of my editors, my fabulous fan group, The Fabinators, my family, and most of all, to you.

—XOXO, Elise

ROOSEVELT RANCH SERIES

ONE

Rex

HE DROVE down the dark road, trying to figure out why he was still in Darlington, Utah, almost two months after he'd deposited Bella back with her one true love, Henry.

Barf.

Love was for idiots.

Or pussies.

Or people who were insanely, sickeningly happy.

Ugh.

Rex was jealous. He knew it. He embraced it.

But that didn't change the fact he wasn't the kind of person who fell in love. Or rather, he didn't *allow* himself to fall in love. He'd seen the way his father had loved his mother—a touching Hollywood scene if there ever was one, filled with so much devotion and affection that when she'd died, his father had changed.

Part of him had died, too.

And so, Rex and Justin had lost *both* parents.

That was the troubling part of so-called happily ever afters.

They never lasted.

Rex sighed because the real casualties in those failed or aborted happy endings were the kids. *They* suffered. *They* lost it all. *They*—

"Fuck!" he said and swerved, almost clipping the car barely pulled over on the shoulder.

No hazard lights flashing. No flares. Nothing but a dark shape silhouetted against the moonlight. Were they trying to get themselves killed?

He slowed and turned around, heading back to the parked car.

His tirade about responsibility was on the tip of his tongue and—*ha!*—if anyone even knew that *he'd* thought the word responsibility, they would have keeled over and dropped dead.

Responsibility and Rex Roosevelt did not belong in the same sentence.

He was the screw-up.

He was the bad guy.

He was pulling over behind the car.

Rex parked behind it and turned on his hazard lights before getting out. He'd extended a hand to knock when he saw the woman inside. Spot-lit by his car's headlights, she looked like an angel with pale blond hair and delicate features.

Or at least from the glimpse he caught, they *seemed* delicate.

He only caught hints of a pert nose, plump lips, and a slender jaw because she was spending a lot of time banging her face against the steering wheel.

Rex hesitated and almost turned away, leaving her to whatever sort of mental breakdown she was determined to have, but just as he'd taken a step back toward his car, his conscience pinged.

The annoying bastard had been all too busy lately.

He sighed but knew he couldn't leave her, and so he blew out a breath, raised his hand, and knocked on the window.

The woman inside jumped.

Her gaze shot to his for one long moment before her eyes slid closed, head dropping down to the steering wheel.

But Rex barely noticed.

Because one look from *her,* and he'd felt like he'd been struck over the head by a two-by-four.

Or maybe hit in the ass by Cupid's arrow.

She was . . . different . . . wonderful . . .

And he wanted her.

TWO

Tilly

"GO AWAY, Y-YOU . . . *YOU!*" she shouted through the closed window of her car.

It was late. It was dark.

Her car had decided it was Satan's spawn again.

And so, no, she wasn't firing on all cylinders when it came to her insult game. Not that her insult game was ever that strong, but circling back to the late, dark, stuck on the side of the road thing—and having watched way too many murder documentaries on Netflix lately—Tilly wasn't about to greet the shadow outside her car with any familiarity.

Especially when all she could discern was that the person crouching to peer into the window of her little sedan was big, with broad shoulders. She grabbed her phone and flicked on the flashlight, shining it in the murderer's—Good Samaritan's—face.

Then almost dropped it in her haste to turn it off.

"Justin?" she asked, identifying her former coworker's husband. Kelly and Justin had been married for a few years, and he was decidedly a good guy.

Think Goody Two Shoes as an alternative to the leading man in a horror flick.

She pressed the button to unlock the car door then popped the handle.

"Sorry," she said quickly. "I didn't know it was you, and I stayed up way too late last night watching this movie, and now it's dark and my car just up and died and—"

Her words cut off.

Because in her haste to exit the car, she'd left the door open and that open door meant that the overhead light was shining, illuminating the space around them.

Illuminating Justin's face.

"I thought your eyes were green," she murmured.

Justin blinked, and it was as though someone had wiped his face clean with a towel, but instead of scrubbing away dirt and grime, her words had rubbed away all traces of emotion.

His expression went blank, blue eyes hardening. "Nope," he said, mouth pressing flat. "In fact, I was born with this pair."

The cadence with which he spoke—arrogant, cool—told Tilly all she needed to know.

"You're not Justin."

"Ding. Ding. Ding." He stepped toward her.

She backed away . . . into the door.

The man didn't stop, just kept moving forward, but just when his chest would have brushed hers, the moment she'd sucked in a huge gulp of air, readying herself to scream, he shifted, nudging her out of the way and dropping down into the driver's seat.

Was he trying to steal her car?

"No," he said with a smirk, nodding in the direction of the sleek sedan that was parked behind her as her cheeks went red-hot with embarrassment at having said that aloud. "I *have* a working vehicle."

What would he want with a dumpy Mazda like hers anyway? It was on the leeward side of two hundred thousand miles, the front seat had a spring that was bent and always poked her as she drove, the radio rarely worked, and . . . well, based on the fact that it was stopped on the side of the road for the umpteenth time in the last few months, it was seriously lacking in the one quality that most people valued in a car this old.

Reliability.

Click.

She jumped, mental diatribe about her vehicle halting. "I tried that—" she said, or rather *started* to say because the not-Justin reached down and tugged on the lever to pop her hood—er, the *car's* hood—then pushed out of the driver's seat. Tilly caught a whiff of his cologne as he went, spice mixed with something earthy.

Her kryptonite.

Sandalwood.

The little *je ne sais quoi* that was the basis for so many scents, both male and female. It rounded out the notes, added depth to something like cinnamon or bergamot, paired well with vanilla and warm black pepper.

A loud banging pulled her out of her mental soliloquy to all things nose-related.

She was Tilly Conner, of the long line of Conners from Darlington, Utah. Who stayed in Darlington, who met their husbands in Darlington, who had tiny humans that grew up in Darlington. Her future was waitressing in Henry's Diner until she met someone she didn't hate—and maybe sort of, even liked—they'd date for the prerequisite one-point-five years, get engaged, get married, pop out some of those tiny humans, then go their separate ways . . . at least in her branch of the family.

And now she was the last of her side.

But regardless of lineage, what Conners from Darlington did *not* do was dream and wish and hope for a different life— especially not one that had her starring as the creator of a line of perfumes and colognes.

Then expanding into hair products. And makeup. And candles.

Nope.

That was exactly what she shouldn't be thinking about.

She *could* go.

But she wouldn't.

"Thinking isn't the problem," she muttered. "It's the hoping that does it—"

A banging noise drove out all imaginings of a different life, in a different place, with different opportunities. She gasped and jumped, clutching the top of the door for balance, shoving all thoughts away, forcing herself to stop acting like a daydreaming child and to focus on the present.

On what was important.

Namely, the fact that she was on the side of the road with a non-Justin, who seemed to be getting very angry with her engine.

"Um," she called over the sound. "What are you—"

"Try it now," the man called, his voice dripping down her spine like honey.

Thighs clenching, fingers still gripping the door, she frowned. "Try what?"

A sigh. Footsteps crunching the dirt and rocks as he rounded the front of the car, slipped around her, and reached over to turn the key in the ignition.

Her engine started up.

And not just the one in her pants, because sweet baby Jesus, his ass in those slacks, the cotton cupping the mounds lovingly, making her fingers ache to touch—

Whoa, girl.

Yes, she'd calmed herself like one of Kelly's horses.

But she'd never been attracted to Kelly's husband. Hell, she'd barely been attracted to *anyone* for the last few years. It was why she *hadn't* made tiny humans, why she was frighteningly single, why—

"Get in the car."

Tilly blinked. "What?"

The man sighed. "I'll follow you home, make sure you get there." When she didn't immediately move, he nudged her again, and this time his fingers brushed the bare skin of her arm.

Sparks.

As in, she felt actual sparks.

Except that was insane.

She was delusional, wrapped up in her bergamot, sandalwood, vanilla haze. She was—

Plunked into the driver's seat, the man's lovely bergamot, sandalwood, and light vanilla scent filling the air around her. He stretched over her, clipped her seat belt in place, put her hands on the steering wheel, then spoke to her like she was the biggest idiot on the planet. "You. Drive. Me. Follow."

Tilly shook her head. "I don't understand how you fixed my car."

A flash of white teeth that threatened to make her stupid. "It's not fixed. It's running. For now." He leaned back, started to close the door. "But you need a new battery and starter."

"Thank—"

The door shut, cutting off her words.

She sighed, used the manual handle to roll down the window. "Thank you for fixing—getting my car started, but I don't need an escort."

He paused, glanced back at her, then shrugged before continuing back to his car.

"What's your name, anyway?" she called as he opened his driver's side and started to climb in.

"Rex," he said, that dripping honey voice now sliding lower. "Rex Roosevelt."

Then, as she was reeling from the confirmation of the truth she'd known deep inside the moment she'd realized he wasn't Justin, Rex started up his car—it purred to life with no protest—and drove away.

The cloud of dust in his wake, the only sign he'd been there at all.

THREE

"STUPID," he muttered. "Stupid fucking idiot."

What had he expected? For her to jump into his arms and declare her eternal love all because he'd banged on her starter?

He snorted.

Yeah, no. Women didn't work that way.

They were transactional, and it was better for all involved if both sides' terms were hammered out in the beginning.

Rex sighed, shifting slightly in his seat because thinking about hammering and banging the beautiful blonde was not good for his self-imposed celibacy. And why was he doing that to himself again?

What did it matter if he fucked his way around the globe?

Oh, yeah. Because he felt like shit afterward.

It had been nice while it lasted, that pussy fog, the bleak numbness that had enveloped him, not caring about anyone other than himself.

And then Kelly.

And feelings.

And a dick that didn't work.

Or didn't want to work for anyone *except* for Kelly.

But he'd gone and screwed things up between him and Kelly way too fucking long ago. She and his twin Justin had found each other in the wreckage Rex had wrought, and they were *happy*.

His newest curse word.

Because everyone was fucking *happy*.

Except him.

"Stop being so sensitive," he muttered, repeating the words his father had told him way too many times growing up—along with "Be a man," and "Feelings are for pussies," and "Women will only destroy you."

So, yup, baggage, for the win.

He was driving at a snail's pace, not breathing until he saw the headlights pull out onto the road behind him, the silhouette of the pretty blonde barely visible in his rearview. She caught up with him pretty quickly, and he continued driving out of town, trying to watch to see where she'd turn off, to make sure she'd make it home safely.

A few months before, he'd have lied to himself, made up an excuse for wanting to know that fact.

Tonight, he didn't bother lying.

He knew he wouldn't get a good night's sleep unless he saw her home.

Darlington was a small town, but he hadn't seen the blonde around, didn't know her name, wasn't on good enough terms with anyone to find out, but just as he was thinking again that he needed to leave and start fresh, the car behind him turned off.

He braked, waiting to see she'd made it up the winding driveway, the headlights drifting orbs of light as they weaved their way up the hill until, eventually, they parked in front of a mostly dark house.

The porch light flicked on—via a motion sensor or someone waiting inside for her—and she bounded up the steps.

Then stopped.

And turned to face the street.

To face *his* car on the road.

She waved, turned for the door, and disappeared inside.

Gone, just that easily.

"Yeah," he murmured, driving forward again. "That's a familiar feeling."

He was being a pest.

But that was Rex Roosevelt's specialty—annoying, pestering, infuriating everyone around him. Luckily, despite the glare his brother was lobbing his way, his rescue of Bella had gone a long way toward thawing the ice Kelly had in her heart where he was concerned.

Well, that and the fact that he'd made it a point to have Abigail and the twins refer to him as Uncle Rex—the twins because he was truly their uncle, and Abigail because while he might have provided one half of her DNA, Rex had never been anything like a father to her.

That was where the infuriating portion of his personality came in . . . or perhaps, disappointing.

Or maybe the best description yet, failure.

And Justin saving his ass, yet again.

Taking care of Kelly, stepping in, falling for the only person Rex had ever felt anything for. But he hadn't felt enough. He knew that now. After he'd returned, thinking he might be able to win her back, he'd seen Justin with Kelly, seen how perfect they were for each other, how they hadn't been trying to take and take and *take* from each other. As opposed to him trying squeeze every bit of satisfaction out of his partners and then never finding it to be enough.

Because he was lacking something inside.

Broken. Missing. Empty.

Jax, Justin's little boy and Jesse's twin, hurtled a toy car off the edge of the table. It clattered to the floor, making Rex wince and focus back on the subject at hand: trading empty, missing, and broken for mischief.

"I just don't see why we can't have ice cream for breakfast," he said, attempting to keep his lips from curving. "We all know that it will be much less messy than Justin making pancakes."

Kelly's eyes twinkled. "True," she said, stooping to pick up the car. "But now you're threatening my stash of mint chocolate chip, and them's fighting words."

Rex lifted his hands in the universal sign of surrender. "Even I wouldn't dare to do that. I know how much you love your mint chocolate chip."

She dropped a handful of cereal in front of Jesse and Jax then a bowl of yogurt in front of Abigail in that easy, efficient way she had. It was the same with the horses, whether it was a handful of them or the several dozen they now housed on the ranch. Kelly could always handle multitasking without missing a beat. This horse needed his medication. Another's favorite snack was apples. Still one more never failed to miss an opportunity to nip. She'd been able to rattle that off to him with her arms full of tack while saddling one horse and passing treats to another.

And she was an even better mother.

Abigail looked exactly like her with the exception of having the Roosevelt eyes. The same eyes Justin had but Rex didn't. Lucky, that. No trace of him. And while they might share that DNA, Rex didn't feel anything fatherly toward her. Maybe once upon a time, he'd thought that perhaps . . .

But he'd let that go.

She belonged to Justin.

Abby scooped up a spoonful of yogurt and shoved it into her mouth. "You're silly, Uncle Rex." Some of the white viscous liquid dribbled down her chin.

He wrinkled his nose and picked up a napkin from the holder in the middle of the table, grabbing the square of paper, then belatedly realizing he'd recognized the painted clay monstrosity from his childhood.

"Where'd you find that?" he asked lightly, wiping Abigail's chin. "I thought Dad had burned it."

Justin's eyes held a note of emotion that Rex didn't like. He held Rex's gaze for a long moment then returned to mixing pancake batter and generally making a giant mess of the kitchen. "Turns out that there was a lot of stuff in storage. Dad sent it over after Abby was born."

"Ah."

Kelly set a bowl of berries, granola, and yogurt in front of Rex, and his heart clenched in regret when he realized she'd remembered his preferred breakfast. "Because it will take Justin an hour to make enough pancakes for all of us."

"Hey! I—" Justin said, but Kelly cut him off with a kiss.

Regret, Rex thought. *Not want.*

He didn't want Kelly any longer, but he sure did regret hurting her.

FOUR

Tilly

HER ALARM CAME WAY TOO EARLY.

She hated working the morning shift, but she hated it all the more when she'd stayed late to cover the evening shift the night before.

"Ugh," she groaned, blearily reaching for her cell and attempting to press the "Done" button. Not "Snooze" because fuck if she wanted to deal with the incessant ringing in nine minutes.

Nine. Not ten. Not five.

Nine.

Her cell slipped out of her hands and fell to the floor with a sickening *crack*.

Hardwood floor meeting glass-covered cell phone was never a good thing, but it was even *less* of a good thing when said cell phone was out of its protective case because the fucking wireless charger didn't charge with the bulky plastic surrounding it. And since Tilly was about as good with technology as a bull in the proverbial china shop . . .

That *crack* meant her brand-new cell phone that she'd splurged for now had a lovely fissure right down the middle of the screen.

Not on the back. On the front. In the middle.

"Fuck my life."

She should have put that money into fixing her car. Instead, she'd splurged and . . . *le sigh*. Because as things had often done in her life, they'd gone wrong.

Since her cell was still incessantly blaring, Tilly shoved her bangs out of her face and slipped out of bed. Two jabs at the screen and she managed to silence the ringing before shoving it back into the indestructible case. Then it was time for her to stop grousing and move.

She was one of those people who didn't like to build extra time into her morning routine. She wanted to sleep as late as humanly possible, then hurtle herself out of bed and into the shower. No washing her hair, because her mane of blond locks took way too much effort to dry for zero-dark thirty in the morning. Rather, she simply waited impatiently for the shower to heat, hopped in, and washed up as quickly as possible, then with slightly more awake hands, fumbled her way into her uniform.

Bypassing her kitchen—it was too early to be hungry for breakfast and Henry would cook something for her that was way better than anything she could cobble together once the morning rush passed anyway—Tilly ran out onto her front porch.

This was the moment she typically ran across the darkened front yard—hello, scary murderers and freezing cold Utah mornings—to her car.

Just not this morning.

She stopped dead—no pun intended—on the second step.

"What the *fuck?*"

Her car was gone.

WALKING IN THE DARK, mind full of scary thoughts and images, did not do a girl well.

She'd called Henry to tell him she would be late but would be in as soon as possible. As usual, he'd been understanding when she'd told him that she had car trouble—*ha*, a missing car still counted as trouble, right? He had offered to give her the morning off to deal with her car, but she needed the money from her shift . . . especially if she might need to buy a new one.

Sighing and mentally adding a brand new vehicle to her already stretched budget, Tilly picked up her pace. She lived on the outskirts of Darlington, but luckily her hometown wasn't what one would call big. It would take all of twenty minutes to get to Main Street, where Henry's Diner was located.

By then, the restaurant would be slammed, every booth crammed with Darlington natives, plates piled high with fluffy pancakes and delicious omelets, perfect triangles of freshly baked bread, courtesy of the lovely Isabella.

Henry's better half was beautiful, inside and out, and an amazing baker, to boot. It would be enough to make Tilly hate her, if not for the whole beautiful on the inside thing.

Because Bella was amazing, and nice, and talented . . . and perfect for Henry.

So no hating. Only love and . . . the slightest bit of jealousy.

Because once upon a time she'd believed in happily ever afters. Then reality had struck and she was back home, in debt up to her eyeballs—though she was slowly making progress in paying it off—and, perhaps most depressing of all, she was alone. All alone.

Wrinkling her nose, Tilly wrapped her jacket more securely around her and quickened her pace.

Winter was coming.

A snort, though it was the truth.

The leaves had turned, the nights had come earlier, the days had grown cooler and shorter. Halloween was in a few weeks and then a fresh hell would begin.

The Holiday Season.

Such a fucking pain in the ass when a girl was alone and single.

"Pity, pity party," she muttered, rounding the corner where her car had been an asshole the night before. The sun was still hidden behind the hills in the distance, but it was beginning to rise, making their tops look like someone had run an orange highlighter across their rounded domes.

It was beautiful and also a good reminder for her to keep moving.

The minutes were flying by, and she'd never get them back.

"Don't I know that?" she muttered and trudged on.

FIVE

Rex

HE FELT his phone buzz and pulled it out to check if it was the message he'd been waiting for.

Then felt his cheeks crease when it was.

There was one benefit of throwing money around. People jumped and often jumped high.

Rex still didn't know what had persuaded him to make the call late the night before, the one that had offered an obscene amount of money to the local mechanic to tow the angel's car to his shop to fix it.

But he *had* and, in fact, had paid more than the actual rust bucket was worth to replace the starter, the ignition, several important belts, one engine rod, and a broken spring in the front seat. Expensive, but Dale, the mechanic, had come through. And if Rex were being completely honest, fixing the car was the lesser of two evils . . . especially when his first instinct had been to buy the woman a brand-new car.

Didn't even know her name and yet was willing to spend thirty grand on a new vehicle.

Brilliant thought, Roosevelt.

Rex sighed then typed out a thanks, asking the mechanic to drive the car back to the woman's house. She'd been working very late the evening before and so hopefully would still be sleeping or at the very least, had seen the note he'd instructed Dale to leave behind.

Last thing he needed was the woman reporting her car being stolen.

Despite his role in Bella's return to Henry and Darlington, the sheriff's office still wasn't his biggest fan. The head detective was Kelly's brother-in-law and not quick to forgive Rex.

Not that he could blame him.

Rex's phone buzzed again.

Already dropped off. Note still there and not a peep from the house. The total with parts will be—

To which, Dale added a monetary amount that was obscene, but marginally less than the price of a new car. He typed a reply, promising to drop the payment by in a couple of hours, and then pocketed his phone and forced himself to focus on the task at hand—namely, cleaning up the kitchen mess that was the result of Justin's pancakes.

The happy family of five had taken off for the barn, coaxed out by Rex, three sets of sticky faces and hands trailing their parents. Knowing Kelly, a morning check and feed of the horses had already been completed, but she'd spend several hours assisting the ranch hands with feeding, exercising, and keeping a close watch on their highly valued horses.

She'd turned this operation into something very special.

No thanks to him.

Rex shook his head, shoved the circling emotions down—because he really needed to stop being a pathetic pussy—then got to work on the dishes. It was almost worth it, having to wash the ridiculous amount of dishes, just to have witnessed Justin's face when he had offered.

Pure, unadulterated shock.

Punctuated by pancake batter above his right eyebrow.

Of course, there was karmic intervention for his amusement . . . in the form of a griddle caked with bacon grease that he spent the better part of thirty minutes scrubbing clean, so by the time he managed to escape it was nearly lunchtime.

Kelly and company were making their way up to the front door as Rex emerged from the house. While she offered to make him a matching heart-shaped PB&J sandwich to go along with Abigail's lunch—and really, how the little girl could be hungry after the huge amount of pancakes she'd consumed less than two hours before was beyond him—he turned down Kel's offer and headed to his car.

Justin was chasing the twins around the front lawn, but Rex didn't miss his brother's shoulders relaxing when he announced his impending exit.

"Bye, Roosevelt clan," he called lightly, really good at pretending that he hadn't secretly wanted to stay.

He liked being around Justin and his family, enjoyed the noise and chaos, interspersed with laughter, tears, and the occasional meltdown. It reminded him of when his mom had still been alive.

But as much as he wanted to soak up every moment, Rex knew he was nothing more than a complication—fine, an *annoyance*—to them.

Things would never be the same.

He'd ensured that.

"I'll be heading back out of town soon," he announced to no one specifically. "Let you all get back to your life."

"Rex—" Kelly began, but her words were cut off when Abigail launched herself from the front porch. She sprinted toward him, little legs pumping faster than he would have thought possible.

"Don't go, Uncle Rex!" she said, and he was surprised to see tears in her eyes.

His heart clenched. "I—"

He didn't do kids, didn't know how to respond . . . to someone wanting him to stay. Or at least, not because they wanted *him* to stay and not his money or his father's business connections.

She sniffed and threw her arms around his waist.

"I—" he started again and stopped. "You're probably hungry," he eventually settled on. "You should go eat that sandwich your mom is going to make you."

Green eyes, so like his brother's, narrowed in his direction. "Mommy says you like to run away." Her gaze was penetrating. "Don't."

And now this was getting really freaking weird.

"I'm not going anywhere," he found himself saying. "Except into town for a bit."

A nod.

"Good." She turned to the house. Stopped. "Because you and Daddy need to make up." With that proclamation, she flounced into the house.

Rex turned to Justin. "How old is she now?"

"Four." A beat. "Going on forty."

His lips twitched. "She reminds me of Mom."

Justin nodded. "Yes, she does."

When the silence stretched for a few beats, Rex nodded, propelled his ass into motion, and hightailed it for his car. This time there wasn't a tiny green-eyed cherub to stop him from buckling in and taking off down the driveway.

But that didn't mean there wasn't an angel to stop him in his tracks just around the corner.

SIX

Tilly

HER FEET ACHED, and her hair smelled like eggs.

Scrambled. With a touch of cheddar, sour cream, and bacon.

The perfect combination for an omelet in her opinion, but definitely not her preferred shampoo scent. She shook out her long blond locks as she walked, another crumb of bacon falling to the road. Her house was ten minutes out, her pace much slower than that morning.

Panic and fear had fueled her steps, and she'd made it into town in record time.

Thank her overactive imagination for that small miracle.

Now, she'd worked the morning rush . . . or maybe it had worked *her*. Because besides the omelet hair she now sported, courtesy of a toddler who'd launched her mother's breakfast in Tilly's direction with unerring accuracy in the middle of a major temper tantrum, her shirt was grease-stained, her cell phone had given its final goodbye thanks to an overturned glass of orange juice, and—

She was tired.

So damned tired of everything.

She hadn't even gotten a chance to call the police depart-ment about her car, and seeing as how she didn't have a house phone any longer, she wondered how in the heck she was going to do that without a cell.

Could she Skype them? Facebook message Kelly's sister, Melissa, since her husband was the lead detective in town?

Did detectives even track down stolen cars?

Weren't they supposed to go undercover and arrest people? Or at least, that was what Rob had done several years before—taken down a huge drug ring and corrupt government agents.

Finding her dumpy little car with two hundred thousand miles on it couldn't be much of a priority.

She wasn't much of a priority.

"Enough," she muttered, kicking a rock and watching it roll down the road. "Enough moping and whining and being tired all the time." She kicked another. "Enough being defeated. Enough of this fucking town and its history and enough of—"

Here, two things happened.

First, a tear escaped her eye.

Tilly had been fighting the salty little fuckers, blinking back against the stinging, trying to drum up some mad instead of the sad that had dominated her life for the last years.

Because she was damn tired of sad.

She succeeded in drumming up the mad and it came on rapidly, raging through her with all the fury of a forest fire. With a snarl—or perhaps a full-bellied, furious scream—she kicked another rock.

And then the second thing happened.

The rock sailed through the air, flying up in a perfect arc until . . . it crashed right into the windshield of a sleek black sedan coming around the corner.

Crack.

The car swerved, brakes screeching as it came to a halt on the shoulder.

Tilly had frozen, her hands over her mouth, for one horrible moment before starting to run. To her credit, she ran *toward* the car, rather than away from it. "Oh God," she muttered. "I could have killed somebody. Shit. *Shit.*"

The windshield had a giant divot in it, several cracks already spiraling out from the center, but thankfully the rock hadn't actually made it through the glass. Sun in her eyes, but concern growing as no one emerged from the car, she reached for the driver's door and yanked furiously on the handle.

It didn't open for several long moments, the only noise the car's engine and her labored breathing. She tugged on the handle again—

Click.

The door unlocked and seeing as she was mid-tug, it flew open.

She landed in a heap on the gravel-covered shoulder, barely registering the sting of her backside and palms as they made contact with the sharp rocks.

Because then, he stepped out.

Him.

Justin's brother.

And fuck her life, that was just absolutely perfect.

SEVEN

Rex

THE ANGEL SITTING in the road, covered in dust and tears, probably should have looked much less angel-like, but instead, she was even more beautiful in the light of day than she'd been the previous evening.

He held his breath as he surveyed her, starting at her toes—sturdy, comfortable sneakers—going to her legs—tight jeans with a rip over one knee—and up to her torso—a shirt from Henry's Diner, identical to the one she'd been wearing the night before. She must be going to work.

Rex frowned.

Had her car not started again?

Dale had better not be fucking with him.

But just as he pulled out his cell to give Dale a piece of his mind, the angel pushed herself to her feet, sighed, then straightened her shoulders and sighed again. She came over to him and stuck out her hand.

"I'm Tilly," she said, hazel eyes meeting his. "And I'm so

sorry. I'll pay for your windshield. I shouldn't have—" She broke off, cheeks reddening. "Well, I shouldn't have been kicking rocks."

He lifted a brow, amusement curling through him at her contrite words. "Why *were* you kicking rocks?"

She shook her head. "Let me give you my number. I'm happy to pay for whatever damages I—"

"Why were you walking to work?" he interrupted.

Tilly, and for some reason that name seemed to fit her perfectly, froze. "Um . . ." Then she wrinkled her nose, and he had the oddest urge to lean forward and brush his lips across the freckles there. "Well, my car was stolen this morning."

Rex blinked. "What?"

"I know, right?" she said. "I don't know who would want that old rust bucket, but I woke up this morning and it was gone. I was thirty minutes late for my shift because I had to walk in."

Walk in?

He took a closer look at Tilly, saw what he'd missed the first time. The shirt wasn't clean and . . . neither was her hair?

Reaching up before he could stop himself, he plucked a piece of green out of her hair. "Is that an onion?"

She flicked it from his fingers. "Chive. There was this little girl who—" She seemed to shake herself, and Rex found that in that moment, he would have given a whole lot to hear the rest. "Never mind. You don't need to hear about my morning. I've already inconvenienced you twice in as many days. My cell is—"

She'd pulled out her phone and froze, cheeks getting even pinker.

"What is it?" he asked, more than a little intrigued about this woman and her reactions.

A rueful smile curved her lips. "My cell is dead."

"Ah." He smiled back. "How'd that happen?"

"Electronics and orange juice don't mix."

"Ah."

"I—" She broke off. "I can give you my email?"

Amusement boiled up in his veins and Rex smothered a smile. "Email is fine." Not that he had any intention in allowing her to pay to replace his windshield, but he also wasn't going to give up any avenue for contacting her, especially if her cell was dead. He made a mental note to take care of that as well and handed her his phone. "Go ahead and put it in." A beat. "You might as well put your cell in, too. The insurance company might need it."

She winced but spent the next twenty seconds plugging things into his phone before handing it back. "I really am sorry."

He tugged the end of her ponytail. "It's not a big deal."

A nod as she shoved her hands back into her pockets and turned away.

"Can I give you a ride?"

She spun back around. "Oh, no. I couldn't possibly—"

Rex wrapped his hand around her elbow, cutting off her protests and leading her toward the passenger's side of his car. "Let me at least drive you home," he said. "I can't just leave you on the side of the road. I'm not a total creep."

"Just kind of one."

Burn.

But he couldn't deny he'd heard that before, more than once even. "True enough," he said, nudging her into the seat.

Tilly had frozen, cheeks turning bright red, hands over her mouth. Rex simply tugged her right arm down, brought the seat belt across her torso, and buckled her in.

Then he closed the door and paused. Breathed.

Once. Twice. *Enough.*

Rounding the front of his car, he tucked down the biting words he wanted to snap back, shoved away the hurt feelings. Numbing coldness swept through him, cooling the burning sensation in his gut, the warmth that had been steadily filling his heart over the last months.

He tugged open the door, plunked into the driver's seat.

Pressing the button to start the ignition, he kept his gaze forward as the car rumbled to life. But when he reached down to shift it into gear, Tilly's delicate voice filled the air.

"I'm sorry."

He shrugged. "It's fine."

"No," she said fiercely. His gaze shot to the right, locked with her beautiful hazel eyes, and it was hard to hold on to that numbness, so damned hard. "It's *not* fine. You rescued me last night, and I repaid you by ruining your windshield."

"It's nothing."

A shake of her head. "It was something to me, and . . ." She paused, sucking in a breath before the words seemed to burst out of her. "It's just, I know something of what it's like to be judged and found lacking. I shouldn't have—" She broke off and nibbled at the corner of her mouth.

"How could anyone find you lacking?"

An honest question, albeit a blurted one that was based more on instinct than actually knowing her. She was a good person. And considering he *wasn't*, Rex figured he was a good authority on knowing when someone wasn't like him. *Thank fuck* she wasn't like him.

"You should buckle up," she said softly.

"What?"

She shifted, one second in her own seat, the next her blond ponytail was in his face, her breasts against his chest. Her scent was a combination of roses and a multitude of food smells—

which should have been off-putting but somehow was intoxicating. He inhaled deeply, felt the *eau de Tilly* sink into his pores.

Click.

She sat back.

He blinked.

"There," she murmured. "Now, you're safe."

Rex didn't believe that for a second.

EIGHT

Tilly

THE DRIVE to her house was only a couple of minutes, but the guilt was eating her alive.

Such an asshole.

As in, *she* was the asshole here.

Rex turned up her driveway, gravel pinging the undercarriage of his expensive sedan. Great. Now she probably needed to figure out a way to budget for a paint job, too.

She turned to face him as they slowed at the top of the hill, another apology on the tip of her tongue.

Then she saw her car.

Her. Car.

Parked exactly where she'd left it the night before, right next to her front porch.

"What the fuck?" she muttered.

Rex pulled to a stop and one brow lifted. "You kiss your mother with that mouth?"

"I would," she said, shock making her lips loose. "If she were still alive." She didn't stay to witness his reaction. Instead, just pushed out of his sedan and walked over to where her beater was parked. Which was the moment she saw the sign on the front porch post.

Don't freak out. I brought it to the shop to fix it up.

—Dale

"What the fuck?" she muttered again.

"Just to be clear," Rex said from very close behind her, the liquid honey of his voice heating her from the inside out, "I'm not opposed to cursing. You do you, sweetheart."

Her breath caught. "Then why bring it up at all?"

"Because hearing the word fuck from your pretty lips is beyond hot." Tilly swallowed hard, but before she could formulate a response to that, he went on. "So, I'm guessing you missed"—he nodded at the piece of paper taped to her porch post—"the note this morning?"

"Unfortunately, it was dark when I left, and I didn't see it."

"That sucks."

A nod. "Though, I guess I don't need to call the police and report my car being stolen."

Half his mouth curved up. "I see it now."

Tilly's brows drew together. "See what?"

"You're a bright side."

"What?"

"You're one of those people who always sees the bright side."

It took a heartbeat for his words to process, but when they did, she couldn't stop the hysterical laughter from bursting free. It ripped out of her, made her eyes fill with tears, chest hiccupping, and knees wobbling. She staggered a few steps forward and dropped onto the edge of her porch. If he only knew. *Oh God,* if he only knew.

One minute, or maybe five minutes, perhaps even an eternity passed before she managed to get herself under control.

And the first thing she saw when she glanced up was Rex. He was leaning against a post opposite her, blue eyes swimming with curiosity.

But he didn't ask.

Just extended a hand and held out a handkerchief.

An honest to goodness linen handkerchief.

"Who *are* you?" she asked, taking it and blotting her eyes.

"Funny," he said, a smirk playing at the edges of his beautiful mouth. "I was going to ask you the same thing."

"I'm just a girl," she said quietly. "A stuck, small-town girl."

"Why are you stuck?"

He couldn't begin to understand, this man who was born into obscene wealth, who'd never had to worry where his next meal might come from, who never had to struggle for anything in his entire life.

"Some people aren't free to flit around the world." She sighed. "Some people have responsibilities."

"And by that, you're inferring I don't have any?"

His tone was deadly, quiet with an edge of frost.

She opened her mouth, ready to backtrack her words, but then thought, *Fuck it all*. Because dammit, no. He didn't have any responsibilities. He wasn't Justin. He'd appeared in town, wreaked havoc, and left. And from what she knew, that was his M.O. "Yes," she said. "That's exactly what I'm *inferring*."

A flash of white teeth. "Well then, angel, I'd say you're right." He pushed to his feet and came close enough that her lungs strained with the effort to keep her breathing steady. His hand lifted, and suddenly she was inundated with the scent of Rex.

That fucking glorious mix of sandalwood and bergamot.

And cinnamon.

It was most definitely cinnamon.

She inhaled, trying to capture it in her memories, holding on to the scent to study later. Why the mix of common ingredients smelled so fucking good on Rex Roosevelt.

Probably the old money.

That was enough for her to snap herself out of the scent fog.

At least until his fingers drifted into her hair, sliding gently through the strands, sending a shiver down her spine, and turning the scent fog into a *Rex* fog. Fingers drifted along her nape, up to the crown of head, and then paused.

"You really are the most beautiful woman I've ever seen." A beat. "Even with chives in your hair." His fingers moved in quick succession, plucking at her scalp several times. He tossed his bounty to the ground, hesitated for a long moment that had her holding her breath, then stepped back. Two seconds later, he was in his car, dust cloud in his wake as he drove down the driveway.

About thirty seconds after he'd disappeared from sight, Tilly reached into her purse for her keys.

She found them easily.

Unfortunately, her orange juice-soaked cell phone was nowhere to be seen.

Even more unfortunately, she knew exactly where it was.

Sitting on the plush leather seat of Rex's car.

Perfect. Just fucking perfect.

NINE

Rex

HE STILL WASN'T sure why he'd done it.

It being doing something not selfish for the first time in his life.

Which was quite possibly an exaggeration, though not by a whole lot, and it didn't do anything to explain why he all of a sudden had emotions and longings and—fuck him senseless —*feelings*.

And *that* was definitely a curse word in his mind.

Roosevelts didn't have feelings.

Except, his brother did. His father had. So maybe it wasn't that Rex didn't have feelings, so much as he preferred to avoid them at all costs . . . because they made him vulnerable.

"I've been hearing too many of those fucking podcasts Kelly is addicted to," he muttered, though not altering his destination. They were filled with all sorts of Millennial bull-shit about self-affirmations and embracing one's emotions. There must be some damned good subliminal messages in them.

Or . . . maybe he was tired of being so fucking alone all the time.

Rex paused, hands clenching the steering wheel for a heartbeat before he brushed off the thought and kept driving. He had important things to do.

Fine.

One important thing to do.

He turned into the small strip mall on the edge of town, thinking it was lucky there was only one cell service provider that worked in the area. Made his next task easier.

And easy he was comfortable with.

Doing something nice for someone without expecting something in return . . .

"Enough," he growled, snatching up the cell and marching into the store. He strode up to the counter, plunked the phone onto the counter, and demanded to see a manager.

There.

That was Rex Roosevelt.

A slender man with bright red curls came out of the back. "Is there a problem, sir?" he asked tentatively.

"Yes." He shoved the cell forward an inch. "Got doused in orange juice this morning. I need an exact replacement."

Relief crossed the kid's face. "I can do that." He glanced down at the phone. "Be right back with it." Then he disappeared back through the gray swinging door. It had a porthole like a ship, but not even that idiosyncrasy could distract Rex from the question swirling around his mind.

Mainly, why the fuck was he doing this?

Because . . . Tilly.

Because something inside him told him to pay attention.

Because he'd only felt this way once before.

With Kelly.

Sighing, knowing he was being a fucking idiot, but not able

to stop himself anyway, he tapped his fingers on the counter and waited. A woman in the corner kept glancing over at him, lips curved as she tried to catch his eye. But that particular type of interaction could only go two ways—she either wanted to fuck him or she thought he was Justin.

And both possibilities would end in disappointment.

Eventually, she stopped trying to get his attention, and he breathed a sigh of relief. The kid came out from the back—Jeremy, Rex realized was his name. Look at that, he could read a nametag.

Kudos to him.

Kudos?

Fuck him. He needed to get out of this town before he turned into even more of an idiot. *Kudos.* Holy fucking shit. He was losing his damned mind. Jeremy held the box toward him, as though expecting Rex to inspect it.

Rex was too trapped in *kudos* thoughts. He took the briefest glance, saw it appeared to be an identical phone then pushed his own cell with Tilly's number on the screen. "Set it up for this account please, but"—he tugged out his credit card—"pay for it with this—"

"Justin?"

Fuck his life.

He didn't turn until Jeremy took his card and started the ungodly long process at the computer that seemed to accompany any trip to a cell store.

Then, very slowly, he rotated to face the woman. She was beautiful, with a mane of chestnut hair and nice lean legs. And great, now he sounded like Kelly describing her horses. Next thing, he'd be describing her flanks.

"I just wanted to say thank you for helping with Kaycee yesterday. I don't know what I would have done without you." She smiled. "It's only a sprain, like you thought, but this mama hadn't been through that before and . . ." Her lips flattened out. "Are you okay? I didn't mean to interrupt you, I just thought—"

So tempting to snap back, to ruin the perfect image of his perfect brother.

But feelings.

Fucking feelings.

Rex forced his lips to curve. "I'll be sure to let Justin know." He extended his hand. "Rex Roosevelt. Justin's twin."

"Oh." Her jaw worked for a second. "I didn't realize you were still . . . um, that's to say, I didn't know—"

He put her out of her misery.

"I'm in town for a few more weeks." A beat. "I'm glad Kaycee isn't badly injured. I'll let Justin and Kelly know."

Her face paled at the mention of Kelly's name. *"Don't.* I shouldn't have bothered—"

"It's no bother. Abigail and the twins are putting me through my uncle paces this afternoon. They're trying to get me back up on a horse." He kept his tone light, though with a deliberate emphasis on *uncle.*

The woman's face was gray now. "I—uh—"

He put her out of her misery. "I swear they're going to try and get me up on Theo." Theodore was widely known as the most temperamental horse at the ranch, and he'd more than earned his reputation. Hell, the last time he'd been in the barn, Theo had tried to take another bite out of him and had nearly succeeded. The only person he liked was Melissa—Kelly's sister —and Rex was half-convinced that was only the case because Theo had gotten to play hero with her and just liked to play up his prowess.

And now he sounded like Kelly again, anthropomorphizing horses.

Though, even he had to admit that Theo had enough personality for ten people.

Kaycee's mom laughed and it was tinged with panic. "Great. Okay. Well . . . just great." She pointed over her shoulder. "I . . . uh . . . should get back to the phones. Need to pick out a new one."

"That's usually why people come to places like this," he said drolly.

She chucked again, still uncomfortable. "Okay . . . well. Bye."

Rex did her a favor and turned away, watching as Jeremy typed for an inordinately long time on the computer, and by the time the kid had finished with the cell, the woman was gone.

He needed out of this town.

But he'd been saying that for weeks, and still he'd stayed.

Why? For what?

Well, at least that part had now become clear. Because . . . Tilly.

"Here you go, man," Jeremy said, setting the phone down in front of him. "Log into the cloud and your latest backup will download. Do you need a new case?" he asked. "This one is a little . . . sticky."

Since it *was* a little sticky, Rex had Jeremy grab one along with a new screen protector. With the way Tilly was going, he thought she'd probably need it.

Five minutes and twelve hundred dollars later, Rex was out of the store and driving back to Tilly's house, brand new cell in hand. He parked at the bottom of the hill and walked up the winding driveway before depositing it on her porch, propping it up where it would be the first thing she'd see when she came out.

Music blared from inside the house, something pop-tastic that he wouldn't be caught dead listening to, but something that seemed to fit Tilly perfectly.

And then he did something he hadn't done since he was a teenager.

Act like a pervert. Lie, but that was what he was going with.

Rex crept forward and peeked through the window, leaning his head so he could glance through a gap of the white cotton curtains.

The house was small, a tiny living room off to one side with the kitchen right in front of him, a narrow hall with a few doors splitting the two spaces. His heart skipped a beat when he saw Tilly standing there, a tea kettle in her hand and a towel wrapped around her head. She wore a plain gray T-shirt along with pajama pants patterned with unicorns, and he thought it was the sexiest thing he'd ever seen.

That was the moment he really did something he hadn't done since he was a teenager.

Rex rang the doorbell.

The peel was loud enough to cover his steps as he sprinted off the porch and hid around the corner of the house. Inside, the music stopped, and he listened to the little house creak and groan as Tilly made her way to the front door.

Was it even safe if it made that much noise? What if the roof collapsed and Tilly—

The front door opened. "Hello?"

Her voice did that thing again. Feelings.

It swung wider, and Rex was careful to keep out of sight. He heard more than saw her cross the porch, though he did catch a glimpse of her bare feet and the lilac mythical-creature-dotted pajamas.

Still sexy.

Still slowly losing his mind.

But for the moment, he was just going to embrace it.

"What?" she murmured, picking up the phone. "How?" She stood there for a long time, and Rex realized he was too damned old to be hiding along the side of someone's house, crouched in the bushes like some sort of serial killer.

But just as he stood up, ready to announce himself, a whistling sound rent the air. Tilly rushed back across the porch, closing the front door behind her, cutting off the sound of the tea kettle with the panel of wood. A soft click of the lock sliding home was the last thing he heard before the music turned back on.

And Rex stood there, firmly planted on the outside of Tilly's world, but not able to make himself so much as peer in again.

Familiar. That feeling was so damned familiar.

TEN

Tilly

SHE STARED at the phone like it was a snake.

First the car.

Now the cell.

What the hell was going on?

Her tea was getting cold, that was what, and Rex had simply returned her phone. That was it. Simple explanation. Simple truth.

But if it were so simple, then why didn't he stay and tell her that? Why doorbell ditch? And how quickly had he driven away for his car to be at the bottom of her hill by the time she'd gotten to the door? It wasn't like her driveway was short.

It just didn't make sense.

Or maybe it made perfect sense. Maybe he didn't want to talk to her. See? Simple truth. It just . . . didn't feel simple.

She sighed and poured herself some tea before getting out her box of essential oils and getting to work. She'd had a big order come through on Etsy that morning. One of the people she'd sold her bath products to at the county fair that summer apparently ran a B&B, and they wanted her to supply them with shampoo, conditioner, lotion, lip balm, and more than a few scented candles.

Twelve rooms worth.

The biggest order she'd ever sold.

Tilly couldn't afford to screw this up, knew that she'd lucked out with her car not actually being stolen—which was a mystery she still didn't understand but also didn't have the mental energy to deal with at the moment.

Dale had fixed it.

Why?

And how much did she owe him?

Shaking her head firmly to dislodge those thoughts, she got to work.

Lip balm first because it was so easy, she didn't understand why people would ever buy it off the shelf. Literally four ingredients and done—beeswax, coconut oil, shea butter, and whatever scent she was feeling.

Or, because the B&B had requested her peppermint hot chocolate version, that variety.

Her kitchen was smelling festive by the time she'd moved on to shampoo and conditioner. They always took a bit longer, as the conditioner, especially, had more ingredients, but she'd managed to knock them both out by bedtime.

She still hadn't looked at the cell phone.

Lie.

She'd looked at it because it had buzzed. Because somehow it had turned on. She just hadn't gotten any further than the home screen, to the message displayed there:

Found your phone, obviously. It was buzzing in my seat. Maybe not as bad off as you feared. Text me back so I know you found it on your porch.

-Rex

Candles.

She needed to make the candles.

But her fingers reached for her phone anyway, and she was surprised when it unlocked right away without FaceID or her passcode or—

Weird.

It prompted her to sign into her iCloud.

Case in point, orange juice and technology didn't mix. Tilly spent a few minutes avoiding Rex's message, instead logging in and making sure her phone was set up just the way she liked it. Her apps and their respective folders needed to be just right, otherwise she'd go—

Avoidance.

She was a master at it.

Her phone buzzed again, and she jumped, cell flying from her hands to crash to the kitchen floor.

"Tilly Conner, you are an absolute mess," she muttered, sending good vibes up to the cellular gods when she scooped up her phone and saw it was unscathed.

Small miracles. Sometimes it was the small miracles in life.

I hope this isn't still sitting on your porch. It's supposed to rain tonight.

"Great." Another mutter, this time tinged with guilt because Rex had gone out of his way for her three times now, and she'd been avoiding him. Why? Well, there *was* the embarrassment factor. He'd seen her at her worst twice now, three times if she counted not replying to his act of kindness of returning her phone. But while her gut was twisting with guilt, that wasn't what was waving the caution flag in her mind.

Rex was dangerous.

He'd left Kelly.

But he'd brought back Isabella.

He'd rescued her twice.

Was it possible he'd changed?

And *that* right there was what was giving her pause.

Men didn't change. Her father hadn't. Her ex-fiancé hadn't. Rex Roosevelt, legendary sleaze, most certainly hadn't.

Except, what if he had?

Tilly sighed in irritation with herself, with the reminder of the man who was creating so much turmoil inside her—she wasn't the type of girl who looked on the bright side, okay? She couldn't afford to be.

So, she bucked up and texted back.

Thank you for dropping it by, Rex.

There. That was good enough. A thanks, if a bit on the cool side. He had gone out of his way and—

Buzz.

Her eyes glanced down before she could stop herself.

How'd you know it was me?

BESIDES THE FACT *that you signed your earlier text message like an elderly person?*

Because I saw your car at the bottom of the hill. Why'd you doorbell ditch me?

A FEW SECONDS passed before his reply came through.

I didn't want to interrupt. You'd had an eventful morning.

Her fingers flew across the screen.

And by eventful you mean I thought my car was stolen, spent way too long attempting to wrestle an omelet away from a very persistent two-year-old and losing, then vandalized your car all before one?

Nothing for a long moment then:

That's a good definition of eventful, yes.

Before she could snarkily reply to that, her phone buzzed again.

How's the hair? Chive free?

Her lips twitched.

Yes. Though you wouldn't believe what I have in it now.

Barely a second before:

Angel, you can't say things like that to me.

Tilly's breath caught in her lungs.

Wax. I was going to say wax. And stop calling me Angel. It's kind of creepy.

Silence in response. She started to set her phone down, knowing that her words were a conversation killer for sure, but just as her case hit the scarred wooden table, her cell vibrated again.

We'll circle back to why you have wax in your hair. Why is calling you Angel creepy?

She wrinkled her nose, decided to leave the candle-making for the following night, and walked down the hall to brush said wax out of said hair.

It just is.

Her brush caught on the wax, and she winced as she worked it through the ends.

At least this time she smelled like peppermint rather than chives and eggs.

Ah. The age-old argument: It just is. I bow to your brilliance.

Tilly rolled her eyes, set the brush on the counter with more force than necessary.

Shut up. I'm not the one using creepy endearments with a woman I barely know.

Buzz.

Fair point. So, how about we solve that problem?

She picked her brush up. Put it down again.

Sure. It's easy. Stop calling women Angel.

A beat before her cell vibrated again.

I meant the getting to know you part of your statement. Not the creep factor.

Her lips twitched. Creep factor?

Well, let's just kill two birds with one stone, shall we? It's creepy and now you KNOW I don't like it.

Tilly had hesitated, her phone in her hand, waiting for Rex's reply for at least a full minute before she realized what she was doing. Waiting on a man. Again. Snorting in disgust, she dropped the cell to the counter and began deliberately brushing the wax from her hair . . . and also deliberately ignoring the message when it came through a little while later.

But eventually she'd brushed her hair until it was wax-free, until it gleamed like one of Kelly's horse's tails.

"Cute analogy," she grumbled. "Thanks, brain."

She picked up her cell from the counter and strode into the bedroom, still ignoring the message, still pretending that she hadn't just been texting with *the* Rex Roosevelt.

But then she saw the words on the screen.

You were like an angel last night.

What the—

Her fingers were typing out a response to that, a demand for an explanation of that bit of nonsense before she realized what she was doing. After quickly deleting the message, she sent the only thing she could.

Thanks for returning my phone.

Nothing then:

Is this where we circle back to the wax in your hair?

Tilly sighed. She knew what she needed to do, and it didn't relate to wax at all.

No, Rex. This is where we circle back to me saying goodbye.

A beat.

How about instead of goodbye, we just say goodnight?

She found that she didn't have the strength to reply to that. Instead, she plunked her phone into the charger, turned off her light, and burrowed under her covers.

Unfortunately, sleep was a long time coming.

ELEVEN

Rex

TWO DAYS LATER, Rex found himself doing something he'd never imagined—striding through the door to Henry's Diner, Abigail holding his hand while Kelly corralled the twins. Justin was running late but was supposed to meet them there, and while Kel could have handled the crew of kids herself, Rex had surprised himself by offering to help anyway.

He'd been at the ranch because it had given him an excuse to drive by Tilly's house when Justin's call had come, and though Kel had told her husband they would just pick another day, the under-five crew was not having it.

Abigail demanded Bella's French toast. The twins banged on the table for, "Muffins. Muffins!"

And like any sane person, Kelly had relented.

Or rather, Rex had caved, promising any manner of baked goods to get the kids to calm down. To which, Kel had sighed then left the room to grab her giant purse and car keys.

"You've got a soft touch, Uncle Rex," she'd said, though her eyes were gentle.

They'd buckled everyone in, and he'd listened to too many renditions of *Wheels on the Bus* en route, and now they were in the diner. He'd stared out the window as they'd driven, pretending to take in the scenery, but really, he'd been focused on not missing their drive by Tilly's house, or the fact that her car wasn't in her driveway.

Two days had felt like an eternity, which was especially ridiculous when he considered the fact that he hadn't even known her three days before.

If her car wasn't in the driveway . . .

Maybe it was parked behind the diner, in the employee lot.

No way for him to check that at the moment, so he had to hope that she was working. Either that or just be content with enjoying some of the fabulous baked goods the kids were looking forward to.

See? He could occasionally ponder the bright side.

They walked over to Kel's booth in the back. As Henry's best friend and a former employee, she had perks, and one of those was a permanent table. Though that table was getting progressively tighter as the kids got bigger.

Henry came over, giving him an even look—infinitely better than the death glares of earlier days, but still not remotely friendly. "Justin coming, too?"

Kel nodded.

"I'll bring the usuals all around then. Rex? What do you want?"

He had no clue, hadn't bothered to eat here before, not when he'd had a housekeeper and cook at the ranch. But he *had* tasted plenty of Bella's food. She'd taken to bringing him her "inventions" after he'd helped her get home, and they were some of the most delicious baked items he'd ever tasted.

"Did Bella make anything fresh today?"

Henry's expression turned incredulous, but his lips tipped

up. "Only brioche, cinnamon rolls, apple turnovers, cheese tarts, and five varieties of quiche. Any of that sound good to you?"

All of it.

But he settled on a cinnamon roll and apple turnover.

Rex would get his sugar fix at the very least.

"Coffee?"

He nodded. "Thanks."

Henry left then returned a few minutes later with drinks for everyone. Kelly stopped him before he went off. "You short-staffed again?"

"No," Henry said. "Tilly's just on her break now that the rush is over."

"Good," Kel replied. "You need to hire someone else."

"I need my star waitress back," Henry teased.

Kel scoffed. "You mean Melissa? 'Cause she's a long way out from waiting tables."

"Considering she's on a book tour for another hit cookbook," Henry said, "I'd agree with you." He grinned. "But I *was* referring to you, brat. Tilly's great, but I miss you around here."

"She's way better at waiting tables than me. Plus, she doesn't puke on customers . . ."

Rex tuned them out as they continued to banter back and forth.

Because he'd noticed something, or rather, *someone*. Tilly had come up behind Henry, pad in her hand, eyes warm and smile on her face.

". . . but she's not you."

That warmth slipped away, that smile became decidedly more forced.

And Kelly for her part—she didn't have a mean bone in her body, would be distraught to know that her words had hurt someone's situation—misread the situation completely. Maybe it was Jesse almost tipping over her cup. Perhaps it was a lack of sleep.

Regardless, she saw Tilly and instead of ending the conversation, she brought the sweet, blond *angel*—take that, creepy vibes—into their discussion.

"Tilly," Kel said. "You've got to convince Henry that you are a way better waitress than me." She laughed. "I was horrible. I could mostly get the right food on the tables, but I was never like you."

Tilly opened her mouth.

Henry spoke first. "You were great. I loved having you here with me."

Kel rolled her eyes. "You just liked having me somewhere I couldn't get in trouble."

"Didn't work out very well though, did it?" he teased. "Still, I give you my award of Henry's Diner's Best Waitress Ever. Right, Tilly? She's got *all* the skills."

"Tilly is way better than I ever was," Kel said. "I'll remind you that she's never even puked on anyone."

Henry waved a hand. "Meh. It was only Justin."

Kel cackled. "Well, I guess she can work up to that."

"Exactly. I'll put it on her evaluation . . ."

Tongue in cheek. As in, this conversation was *all* a joke, poking fun at Kel's subpar waitressing talents. But the problem with inside jokes, with teasing and laughing in that manner was that if a person didn't understand all the context, if they happened to be on the outside looking in, the joking part didn't matter. They either felt left out or they might take that lighthearted ribbing personally.

Especially, if a soft, vulnerable underbelly had accidentally been punched.

And Tilly seemed to choose the second option.

She whirled away, disappearing through the swinging double doors.

Kel and Henry didn't notice.

But Rex did.

He stood up and followed her into the hall, walking past the bathrooms, the kitchen, Henry's office. No sign of Tilly. But the rear exit was slightly ajar, and he found himself pushing through the metal door, stepping out into the alleyway behind the restaurant.

Tilly was there, clad in faded blue jeans and a white diner T-shirt, black apron filled with pens and notepads slung around her waist.

It would have been good if his perusal stopped there.

Preferable for both of them and significantly less messy.

But Rex found he couldn't stop his eyes from locking onto Tilly's face, from noticing the paleness of her skin, her lips. All except her eyes. *They* were slightly reddened.

She turned to face him when the door closed. "I'm fine, Henry. Just tired—"

Her words cut off.

"Hey," he said, prose-writing genius that he was.

"You're not Henry," she said.

"No." A shrug as he leaned carefully against the wall. "I'm pretty sure he's still teasing Kelly about puking on Justin all those years ago."

Tilly did a valiant job of forcing a smile. "It's a good story."

Rex nodded. "Their meet-cute."

Blond brows drew together. "Their what?"

"The way they met." He shrugged. "Every romcom has one. Saving someone from a car because their heel is stuck, bumping into someone and spilling their coffee on them, accidentally texting the wrong person." Another shrug. "Pick your poison. There are oodles of them."

One of those pretty brows lifted. "Oodles?"

He lifted his own in return. "Better than Angel?"

God, she was cute when she wrinkled her nose. "Yes. But just barely."

"You know what they were saying wasn't about you at all, right?" Rex inwardly groaned because when had he become a fucking therapist? He didn't know the first thing about healthy emotional reactions and sure as shit shouldn't be advising someone else on how to feel.

And anyway, he'd managed to distract her for a moment then had brought up the same thing that had upset her in the first place.

Super smooth.

Fucking moron.

Her eyes chilled. "Of course not. I just needed some fresh air."

He should have let the lie stand, but instead—and see above because fucking moron—he blurted, "I thought you just finished your break."

What the fuck was wrong with him?

Why did this woman turn him into an idiot?

"Never mind," he said. "I just wanted to make sure you were okay."

Tilly's expression was bewildered. "I'm fine."

Well, at least he'd distracted her from whatever had made her sad, even if it had been because he was acting insane. Rex nodded. "Okay, great. Well—"

"I wanted to say something," she murmured, touching his arm and stopping him in his tracks when he turned to go. "I should have said it sooner."

"What?" He rotated back to face her, struck again by how beautiful she was.

But it wasn't just her gorgeous cheekbones or the way her

bottom lip was slightly bigger than the top one, nor was it the delicate arch of her eyebrows or the lovely green and gold and brown of her irises. Because while all of those made for a beautiful package on the outside, none of it came close to what he was drawn to on the inside. Vulnerability was normally a turnoff for him—Rex wasn't a rescuer by any means. In fact, usually any slice of weakness made him head for the hills, *a la* him taking off on Kelly.

The biggest weakness of all was attachment.

But though he barely knew Tilly, though he was already feeling more than a little attached, for the first time in his life, he wasn't freaked out by the idea of building those bonds. In fact, he found that every minute with her made him want more—to figure her out, to discover why *her*. Why he was so drawn to this woman when he'd had so many others before and never felt anything like this for any of them.

Tilly worried her bottom lip with her teeth. "I just wanted to apologize and to say thank you for returning my phone. I don't know how you got it working again . . ." She paused, as though waiting for him to confess some mysterious cell phone fixing ability, but Rex wasn't about to push it, wasn't going to lie to this woman who was so different from all the others. Instead, he just studied her, watched her teeth sink into that lip again, the slightest bit of pink creeping along her cheekbones.

"I'm glad you have a working phone again," he said into the silence. There, that wasn't a lie exactly.

Tilly froze, eyes widening. "You didn't." She reached into her apron, pulled out her phone then gasped. "I was so thrown off that I didn't realize before. You. Didn't."

"Didn't what?" he asked carefully.

"You did *not* buy me a new phone, Rex Roosevelt!"

Shit.

"It's not a big—"

"Do not say it's not a big deal," she said, pacing away. "I have insurance. It would have covered it. This phone is stupid expensive. I shouldn't have even splurged for it in the first place and—" She shoved it in his direction. "Take it back. I'll go to the store after my shift and get a cheaper replacement."

He caught it before it tumbled to the ground, shoved it back into her apron. "Keep it," he said. "I can't return it anyway. Save your insurance for a future cell failure. It seems likely that you might need it," he added when she tried to push it into his hands again and he had to scramble to catch it. Her fingers were on his wrist, his hand in her apron pocket as he tucked the phone deep inside when he blew it completely. "Fuck, woman. It's not like I bought you a new car. It's just a phone, accept the damn thing graciously."

So, Rex meant the words.

And though had he not been so frustrated, he might have tried to find a kinder way to say the same thing, he still *meant* the sentiment.

It was just the car addendum he would have skipped.

Her jaw dropped open and she slapped his hands away from her apron.

Since that meant the phone ended up in her pocket, Rex allowed it. And because her poking him in the chest with her finger brought her close enough that he could smell her delicate scent, could see the way her lips flushed bright pink in fury, he allowed that, too.

"Rex. Roosevelt," she gritted out. "You did *not* fix my car."

He shrugged. "According to the note, Dale fixed it."

She plunked her hands on her hips, one foot tapping. "And who called Dale?"

"Does it matter?" he asked.

"Yes, it matters!" she snapped, yanking at the end of her ponytail and pacing away.

He couldn't not follow her, didn't back up when she spun around and nearly plowed into him. "Why?" he said, tone as harsh as hers. "Who gives a fuck? Your car works. Your phone works. I made one stop, one call, threw some money that I could easily afford at your problems and—"

"It fucking matters because I don't know you!"

Rex clenched his jaw tight, biting back the urge to refute that statement because dammit, he *didn't* know Tilly. He knew she wore lilac unicorn pajamas, that she worked her ass off at the diner, and then went home to fulfill products ordered from an Etsy storefront he'd discovered two nights before.

He'd seen her up late in her kitchen, moving back and forth from the stove to the counters, filling bottles, stirring pots—

Fuck, yes. He was still spying on her. A.k.a. Rex was losing his goddamned mind.

But he'd worried. He'd obsessed and—

Fine. He'd made a few calls to some of his favorite luxury bed and breakfasts, all but demanding they start carrying Tilly's line of products. Her stuff wouldn't disappoint, despite his multitude of experience with crap business ventures, he knew at least that much. Now he just needed to talk her into raising her prices and setting up a storefront.

"You don't have to know me," he finally said. "All you have to do is accept that I wanted to do something nice for someone other than myself and move the fuck on."

She stopped, eyes flashing. "You mean accept it *graciously.*"

"Well, fuck yes. That would be nice for a goddamn change."

Tilly stepped toward him, that finger digging into his chest again. "People don't do things for nothing." Her words were sharp, like daggers. "There are always strings. *Always.*"

That statement made him sad.

He didn't want her to have learned that lesson.

He wanted her protected, for her life to be easy, and maybe .

. . maybe he'd done it in a vain hope that she might actually give him a chance.

Despite his reputation in this town.

Despite his royally fucked up past.

Despite—

"I don't have any strings, Angel."

More wrinkles on that cute nose. He wanted to kiss them away. But at least his response seemed to have distracted her from her anger. "I thought we'd cooled the *angel* talk, creeper."

His mouth curved. "If you're pissed at me, I might as well go all in."

Tilly sighed, glancing up at him and reminding his body once more that she was close, so damned close that it would only take the smallest movement to bring their torsos flush, their mouths aligned. A heartbeat passed, and she seemed to sense the same thing he did, freezing in place, voice dropping to a whisper. "All in with what?"

Rex held his breath, considering his options for the first time in his life rather than jumping into the deep end head first.

But that brief hesitation didn't change anything.

Because, in the end, he jumped anyway.

Wrapping his arm around Tilly's waist, he slammed his lips down onto hers.

TWELVE

Tilly

WHAT WAS HAPPENING with her life right now?

She was in the arms of the most beautiful man she'd ever laid eyes on, his mouth was slanting across hers, tongue caressing the crease of her lips, inching inside to stroke along hers.

Tilly Conner, smelling of sweat and eggs and grease, was in Rex Roosevelt's arms, and he was kissing her as though she were the most precious object on the planet.

But only for a moment longer, because the second she rose on tiptoe, the moment she allowed herself to get closer, to feel his chest against hers, to soak in just a little more of his bergamot and sandalwood scent, something in Rex snapped.

His control. His sanity. His—

It didn't matter.

Because suddenly the kiss wasn't soft and sweet and gentle.

It was fucking hot.

His arm banded around her waist, his free hand wove into her hair. He tilted her head back, and Rex kissed her . . . really, *fucking* kissed her. With teeth and tongue and roving hands. With an erection poking into her belly and rough fingers in her hair. With more heat and passion than she'd ever felt before.

She never wanted it to end, just wanted to stay wrapped up in him for an eternity, to feel those flames of desire licking up her skin, sliding through her center, coiling in her stomach, between her thighs.

She wanted him to slip his hand down, to feel how wet she was for him, and—

Tilly needed air.

Gasping, she pulled back, sucking in much-needed oxygen.

Rex let her breathe, though his mouth didn't stop moving. She felt hot breath on her throat then his teeth nipped, making her jump before his tongue darted out to soothe the slight sting.

"Rex," she murmured, not wanting to break the moment but knowing that at any second someone could walk out of the diner and find them.

"Mmm?"

"We have to stop."

"Uh-uh." He tugged the neck of her T-shirt to the side, licked her collar bone. "We don't."

She gasped, fingers coming up to clench his shoulders. Tilly sucked in air, trying desperately to hold on to the one sane thought swirling around the desire and need filling her brain. "But we should anyway."

Rex froze, entire body stiffening as though she shoved a live wire up his—

Before she could finish that thought—which was probably for the best considering its direction—he set her away from him and stepped back. "You go in first."

Cold, cold words from a man who'd been kissing her so hotly only heartbeats before.

"Are you—?"

"My cock is threatening to poke a hole in my jeans, Tilly," he growled. "So, no, I'm not okay." Blue eyes locked with hers. "And you won't be either unless you go. The. Fuck. Back. Inside."

Heat this time. Heat that threatened to make her smile.

But one glance into those baby blues, into the fire roiling just beneath the surface, and she reconsidered. His expression said that he would have her naked and against the diner's brick wall given the slightest provocation, whoever might walk in on them be damned.

She hesitated because, dammit, Rex was sexy as shit and kissed like a dream and it had been so *fucking* long.

"Go," he snapped, jarring her out of her thoughts and startling her into motion.

Tilly hurried through the metal door, emerging into the hallway, heart pounding, lungs sawing, and . . .

Smile on her lips.

Rex Roosevelt.

Hot damn.

SHE SPENT a few minutes delivering plates to Kelly's table since her order was ready, and Henry had apparently gotten too invested in his conversation with his bestie to realize the food was growing cold in the pass.

Something Bella would kick his ass for later, Tilly reminded herself with a smirk as she set the plates of French toast down in front of Abigail.

Justin had arrived, and he swiped his finger through the freshly whipped cream piled high on top.

Part of the reason that Bella's food was so popular with the kids.

She knew her audience . . . and fully understood that her freshly whipped cream was like crack. Which was a euphemism that she would not be sharing aloud with the class. And definitely not with Rex, who seemed to take even the most innocuous words to a whole new realm of dirty. What he would do with cream and crack she couldn't even begin to imagine.

Blueberry muffins with freshly grated hash browns went in front of Jesse, while the chocolate chip muffin with scrambled eggs she plunked down in reach of Jax.

"Careful," she told the little boy. "The plate is a bit hot."

Wide blue eyes—so much like Rex's that it took her breath away—met hers. How had she never noticed before? And such an odd twist in genetics that even though Rex was technically Abigail's biological father, she looked nothing like him, but the little boy was his spitting image.

For the first time, she wondered how he was possibly in Darlington, how he was interacting with the family, playing the role of uncle when Abigail was really his.

It had to be tough to step aside like that.

And it wasn't like Abigail's parentage was a secret, Darlington was the epitome of small town, and gossip spread like wildfire—which was to say that everyone knew exactly who Abigail's father was, and it wasn't Justin.

Not fair, she thought, shoving the uncharitable thoughts aside.

Sperm did not make a father, as she so personally knew, and Justin had been there since the beginning. He was a great dad, and she thought highly of Rex for having stepped back and let Justin and Kel build their family.

If someone wasn't ready to be a father, then sometimes it was better for all parties involved if he didn't try to fill that role.

Or maybe she was thinking of herself and her own father.

Of all the times he'd canceled or hadn't shown up or had

flaked out because he couldn't *handle* it. *Her*. So, yeah. Abigail was lucky to have two parents who loved her dearly along with a fun uncle.

By the time she'd snagged the final three plates and returned to the table, Rex was back, leaning against the wall as Kel and Henry continued to talk.

Justin rolled his eyes, smiling at her, but Tilly had a hard time focusing on anything except Rex. He was disheveled, his hair sporting tracks from her fingers running through it, his shirt wrinkled, lips swollen.

No doubt hers were the same.

It would be a fucking miracle if no one figured out what they had been doing in that alleyway, she thought, panic seeping up inside her.

Yet, at the same time, would it really be so bad?

Hadn't she just been thinking he wasn't a terrible person?

But he was Rex Roosevelt—love 'em and leave 'em, flighty millionaire, more notches in his bedpost that a fucking wood-carver Rex Roosevelt. She couldn't be attracted to him, couldn't want him.

Not if she wanted to escape with her heart intact.

If he was nothing else, then he was dangerous, and if Kel had illustrated only one thing clearly in her entire life, it was that Rex wasn't a man with staying power. He got what he wanted and he got the fuck out and . . .

Tilly couldn't afford to do that again.

Not for a third time.

Just . . . not ever again.

THIRTEEN

Rex

OUTSIDE LOOKING IN, that was the theme of his life, and it was no different watching his brother with his family.

They hadn't even saved him a seat, for fuck's sake.

Justin had just swept in and taken his spot . . . along with his fucking breakfast. Well, that was nothing new, but that apple turnover looked heavenly. And apparently, his brother thought the same because he picked it up from the plate Tilly had situated at the end of the table and took a giant bite, even though she'd also set a plate with Justin's usual omelet in front him.

Fucker.

Tilly flicked a gaze in his direction that he pretended not to see, even though he noticed everything about her, including the kiss-swollen lips and the way her cheeks went pink when she glanced in his direction, but most especially the way she slipped away from the table as quickly as possible when she noticed him staring.

She disappeared through the swinging doors with barely more than a flash of her blond ponytail.

Rex sighed and pushed off the wall. His brother had moved onto his cinnamon roll, and he barely glanced up when Rex came over to the table, Henry having finally departed the table. Abigail had a whipped cream mustache, Justin was in his seat, and the twins were covered with their respective muffins. Rex crouched next to the table to fist bump Abigail then waved at Jax and Jess, thus avoiding chocolate and blueberry coated palms.

Kel's face clouded. "You don't have to go, Rex—" She nudged Justin. "We'll pull up a chair."

"I've got a few calls to make," he told her. "Enjoy the crew."

"But you haven't eaten your breakfast . . ." Her voice trailed off when she glanced down at the crumbs that were all that were left of his apple turnover and cinnamon roll.

"I'm not hungry anyway."

"Oh, sorry," Justin said, finally coming out of his sugar and carb stupor and staring up at Rex. "Was this yours?" It actually sounded like, "Sho, smorry. Smwas fish hors?" but Rex was well-versed in his brother's full-mouthed speech to deduce the words without an issue.

Kelly rolled her eyes, wiping a napkin across the table to clean up the crumbs her husband had spit on the table. "And they say romance isn't dead," she muttered, but her eyes twinkled as she pressed a kiss to Justin's mouth. "Should I wipe your face for you, too?"

Justin slid an arm around her shoulders. "You love me," he teased. "Even in my Hoover mode."

Thinking that sentiment could definitely be applied in a different way from what his brother was implying, Rex called his goodbyes then walked out the front doors of Henry's Diner.

Main Street of Darlington was probably his favorite thing about the small town. Brightly colored buildings lined both sides of the street, each a different shade of the rainbow, but all of them somehow fitting together. Maybe it was the crisp white trim or perhaps the eclectic mix of architecture, but whatever the magic mixture was, it had a way of relaxing him like no other place on the planet.

Probably why he'd decided to sublet one of the apartments over the empty shop just a few buildings down.

He'd stayed all of one night with his brother and Kelly before making the decision to get his own place, however temporary that might be. And because it had been the peak of summer when he'd chosen to stay on and the B&B had been full, subletting his own apartment had seemed the smartest option.

Today's perk was that he didn't have far to walk to get home.

Though later, he'd have to figure out how to get his car.

Darlington didn't exactly have Über.

There. Maybe *that* was what he should do with his life. He'd played at being the screw-up for so long, stepped right into that image and didn't correct anyone—read: he didn't correct his brother—when they'd assumed he'd failed. He wasn't a great businessman like his father or even the noble, hardworking sod like his brother.

A mediocre, fifty-percent successful man, that was him.

Some of his plans succeeded, some crashed and burned. Same as anyone.

The difference, he supposed as he strolled toward his apartment, was the Roosevelt name. Ubiquitous with success and definitely with old money. And . . . the truth was that for a time, Rex had loved pissing off his dad and brother. He'd *wanted* to be the black sheep, going his own way. So, he didn't tell his family that his production company had a hand in the last four Best Picture Oscar winners, nor did he pass along the information that the small startup he'd invested in had received a patent for a lifesaving blood pressure medicine. He shared the horrible documentaries, the failed cruise line that he had merely loaned a friend a few thousand to help settle debts. He bought a failing ranch on a whim from a rancher who wanted to retire but didn't have the means to.

All because he'd like this little strip of Americana.

Rex's persona had one thing right. He was impulsive.

Dropping several million on a ranch and several million more on the horses, falling for the woman who cared for them, and then when things had gotten too serious with Kelly, bailing.

Well, panicking *then* bailing.

But this thing with Tilly was different. Panic was the least of his emotions—needing, wanting, fucking hard as granite any time she was in the vicinity, they were all infinitely more common.

And more . . . she called to a part of him he'd thought hadn't existed.

The Roosevelt Rescue Gene.

His father had it. Justin sure as shit possessed it as well.

Rex had always figured it had skipped over him. Until Tilly, that was. Because from the moment he'd seen her bashing her head against her steering wheel, the pale blue lights of her dashboard haloing her face, he wanted to both fuck and rescue her.

In equal proportions.

Probably that should have made him run away in terror, but instead he felt calm, at peace with the fact that his soul seemed to resonate with Tilly's. Not love, definitely not that treacherous emotion, but more like . . . a woman he could sleep with and then not immediately want to throw out the front door, one who was sweet and hardworking and who'd refuse all the nice things he wanted to do for her.

One who might make his tough as boots, way overcooked pork chop of a heart not wither up and die further.

Pork chops.

Fuck, he hadn't thought about them in ages. Not since his

mother had passed. The one meal she knew how to cook . . . and cook was definitely a loose term for the shoe leather she'd managed to transform those chops into.

It was the reason his father had hired Rosa—the house-keeper and chef that he and Justin had grown up with, who now lived at Roosevelt Ranch—in the first place. His mother hadn't been able to use a stove to save her life, and though she hated what she'd called "a ridiculous expense," her three boys were thrilled to have edible food and a kitchen that didn't smell like whatever she was attempting to burn—*cough*—cook.

Although, Rosa was getting ready to retire and Kel wasn't great in the kitchen either, so perhaps Roosevelt men were only attracted to women whose talents existed outside of the kitchen.

Hmm.

He wondered whether Tilly could cook.

Tilly.

His cock twitched.

Tilly, who'd kissed him back without hesitation, whose fucking incredible breasts had been plastered against his chest, who—

"Rex!"

Was right behind him.

He turned, watched her close the distance between them. She had a gray hoodie slung over her shoulders, a small black purse held in one hand, a box in the other. And fuck, but he might be developing a fantasy for worn-in T-shirts and faded jeans because her diner uniform hugged those incredible curves exactly as his hands longed to. She blushed, that lovely shade of pink creeping into her cheeks as she walked toward him. Probably because his gaze was locked onto her, taking in every inch of deliciousness.

"Hey, Angel."

She stopped, box dropping to her side, hazel eyes sparking

fire. "You know what? Never mind." Tilly spun away, ponytail fanning out behind her as she turned, a little flash of gold on an otherwise cloudy day.

"No." He grabbed her arm. "Why'd you come over?"

A huff and he couldn't lie and say he didn't like the thing that sigh did to her boobs, the slight jiggle even beneath the cotton. "I'm leaving, Rex."

"Because of *Angel*?"

She shrugged. "It's creepy," she muttered, but then her voice changed, dropping in volume, becoming laced with something that sounded suspiciously like vulnerability. And they all knew where Rex Roosevelt stood when it came to this woman and anything approximating vulnerability. "And plus, I asked you to stop."

I asked you to stop.

Why did he think there was a bigger story behind that statement?

Probably because of the haunted look in her gorgeous eyes.

"Tilly." He cupped the back of her neck, met her stare straight on. "I'm sorry," he told her. "It won't happen again."

She shook her head, silky hair sliding over the back of his hand. "What'd you tell me before?" A beat. "Oh, that's right. You do you. It doesn't matter what I want."

Rex scoffed. "The fuck it doesn't." He squeezed lightly when her eyes darted away, bringing them back to his. "*You* matter. What you want matters." She swallowed roughly, then shook her head again. "Sweetheart."

A sigh before she slipped from his grip.

He could have held tight, could have kept her close, but they were in the middle of downtown Darlington and already risking a ride on the gossip train. Rex glanced around, surprised they had thus far gone unnoticed, but draw this encounter out any longer, and they'd be the talk of the town.

"What's in the box?" he asked when she merely stood there and stared at him, shadows in her eyes.

"What? Oh." She thrust it at him. "I noticed that Justin ate your breakfast." A shrug. "So, I brought you some."

He lifted the lid, saw she'd packed him two apple turnovers and a cinnamon roll.

"Bella said you could have the last two," Tilly said, cheeks still pink. "Seeing as you saved her and all."

He snorted. "She did as much saving as I did."

"That's not what I heard."

"I need to go," he said quickly, not wanting to get into his supposed heroics. "I should get home."

Tilly paused, and this time it was *her* turn to study him, and though Rex tried to keep his expression placid, he had the feeling this woman saw way too much: how he was drawn to her, the crazy connection he couldn't seem to shake. How he had so much respect for her, despite just getting to know her, and other . . . deeper feelings.

Danger.

Her mouth curved. "Want a ride home?"

Fuck danger.

He tugged the end of her ponytail. "Sure."

FOURTEEN

Tilly

THEY'D BEEN DRIVING for about ten minutes when Rex abruptly broke the silence and said, "Where are you taking me?"

She frowned, had the sugar from those two turnovers he'd pounded gone to his head? "Um. Home? To the ranch," she added when he continued to look confused.

"What?" He glanced out the window. "Oh. I don't live at the ranch."

She turned right down the road leading out of town. They'd drive by her house in just a couple of minutes. "I didn't mean live," she said. "I meant staying. You're staying there with Justin and Kelly."

"No, I'm not."

Tilly glanced over at him, sure he was messing with her. "What are you talking about? Where are you staying if not the ranch?"

She would have heard if he was at the B&B.

"Above the old bookstore."

Now, she did more than glance over. She stopped the car on the side of the road. Conveniently, this was in front of her own driveway, so she didn't mind blocking it.

"You're living downtown?" she asked, incredulous. "Then why in the hell did you let me give you a ride? You could have walked there in two more minutes."

Rex held up the box. "Baked goods."

She lifted a brow.

He looked like he was trying not to smile. "You offered."

Tilly sighed, plunked her head back against the headrest. "How is this my life?" Then when he didn't reply, she tilted her neck so her cheek was against the headrest and her eyes were on him. "Why do you look so amused?"

"What were you doing in your kitchen so late last night?"

The question took her aback—shock before the creep factor sank in. "How'd you know I was in my kitchen late last night?" she asked carefully, wondering if she might be able to execute some sort of throw the door open and speed away maneuver if his reasoning was as weird as his words.

"I drove by late from the ranch. Saw your light was on."

The correct answer, a perfectly reasonable expectation, and yet it seemed a little too pat.

But before she could ruminate on that, Rex bopped her on the nose. "Not a stalker," he reassured her. "Just curious."

"I run an Etsy shop. Basic toiletries and home goods— candles, air fresheners, soaps, and hair products. Nothing super exciting," she said. "Just filling a few big orders that came in recently."

"That sounds promising."

Her hands tightened on the steering wheel. "I hope so," she told him. "I love Henry, but I don't want to be stuck in the diner forever. I want—" She broke off, stifling the rest of that sentence because she was so far away from being able to think about what she wanted that it was almost comical.

Almost.

Rex's fingers grazed her cheek. "What do you want?"

She almost told him, came a heartbeat within sharing the secret desire in her heart. To make her side-hustle something big and profitable and worldwide. How she'd dreamed it would start online and grow to storefronts. How it might one day allow her to pay off the stifling debts so she could travel or have a house where she wasn't worried if the water heater was going to go out or whether the next big snow might collapse the roof.

But she was lucky. In so many ways.

Thus, as she'd gotten so damned good at over the last two decades of her life, since her seven-year-old's dreams had been so thoroughly shattered, she shoved those dreams down and forced herself to smile.

"Oh," she said, laughing lightly. "I want the same as anyone I supposed. Food, a place to live, some really good, really bad reality TV."

"Really good *and* really bad?"

She shrugged. "It's only really good if it's really bad."

His mouth curved up into a grin that should have been illegal. "And you like things that are bad?"

Since she wasn't going to fall for *that* line, Tilly smirked. "I'm afraid that my enjoyment of bad, bad things ends with scripted reality television."

"Hmm."

Shifting her gaze forward, she prepared to turn the car around. "You can actually just drive me to Kelly and Justin's," he said. "If you don't mind. My car is there since Kel drove me to town."

"Well," she muttered. "Since we're almost there already . . ."

She scanned for cars then pulled back onto the road, heading toward the ranch once again.

"So, a soap-maker and a waitress," Rex said. "Anything you can't do?"

She snorted. "So many things," she told him. "Starting with baking cinnamon rolls that are half as good as Bella's."

"But could you teach me how to make a candle that *smells* as good?"

A pause. No one had ever asked her how she made her products.

"Why would you want to know that?"

He drummed his fingers on the center console, the sharp *rap-rap-rap* drawing her attention to how close his hand was to her thigh . . . and how she wanted it that much closer. *On* her thigh, sliding *up* the inside of her legs, pressing—

"I find that I want to know everything about you."

"*Oh.*"

Not magical prose or a witty response. Just *oh,* after the most beautiful and fascinating man she'd ever met said he wanted to know *everything.*

Perfect.

"But I'll start with your favorite type of flower."

Her hands twitched on the steering wheel. "What?"

"I'll start with the easy questions first."

"Um . . ."

"Do you not like flowers?"

She loved them actually, but the strange turn in conversation had taken her for a loop. "No."

"So, what kind? Roses?"

A shudder coursed through her. That was one scent and flower she couldn't abide by, not when her mother had loved them so violently that it had taken her months to forget the cloying fragrance that had clogged her nostrils in the hospital, that had filled the rooms in her home. It had taken ages to get the smell out of the house.

"Okay, not roses," he said quietly.

"No, not roses," she murmured. "I like sunflowers."

"Yellow?"

"For the sunflowers?" Her shoulders relaxed at his nod. "Yes, I like those. They're cheerful, but I really love the rust-colored ones or the slightly reddened ones you find in the grocery store this time of year. It's so fall and . . ."

"Cheerful?" he supplied.

Surprised, she glanced over at him. "Yes," she murmured. "That exactly."

"Fitting," he said, then spent their last couple of minutes together quizzing her on her favorite food—chocolate, duh—favorite movie—she didn't have one, but was a sucker for super-hero films—and her favorite scent—which gave her ample opportunity to wax poetic about her love of bergamot.

And shockingly, he didn't seem bored out of his mind.

In fact, when she talked about how she paired the fragrances together to make her products, he'd seemed genuinely interested and had actually asked a few insightful questions about her process.

It was the best conversation she'd had in ages.

And she hadn't even asked him a question about himself, but when she parked in front of the ranch and opened her mouth to apologize for monopolizing their time, he placed a finger over her mouth and seemed to know what she was thinking before her apology crossed her lips. "I wouldn't have asked if I didn't want to know."

"Well," she said, the slightly roughened skin of his finger making her mouth tingle, "I want to know those things about you, too."

His smile bordered on a smirk, but she liked it anyway.

She also liked when he moved his hand and replaced it with his lips . . . and tongue. He kissed her for ages, mouth working against hers, the slick darting of his tongue slowly driving her insane, but eventually he pulled back, both of them sucking in huge gulps of air.

"Good," he said.

She frowned. "Good, what?" The kiss was more than good, it was fucking off the charts.

"Good, you want to know those things," he said, pressing one more kiss to her lips. "Because I can tell you when I come over to learn how to make a cinnamon roll candle tomorrow." Then, as though he hadn't just dropped a giant bomb, he popped the door handle and slipped from the car.

Dumbfounded, she didn't immediately drive away.

The knock on her window made her jump, but she rolled the pane down when he gestured for her to do so. But by the time she'd cranked it open—this car was from the Stone Age when electric windows were just a pipe dream—he had a scowl on his face.

"Did you really have to do that by hand?"

The gleam in his expression was becoming familiar. "Don't you dare buy me a new car, Rex Roosevelt!"

"It would have automatic windows," he said.

"No." She narrowed her eyes. "This works fine, and you've already done way too much for me. Now I have a reliable car *and* phone, so *no more*." Maybe if she was firm enough, he'd listen because that gleam was calculating, and she didn't need to owe this man any more favors.

He pouted for a moment before his tone went cajoling. "You could have seat warmers."

Oh. Now that would be nice.

No!

She glared. "Stop it, Roosevelt. You will not woo me with

seat warmers and automatic windows, or I won't teach you my magical mastery of candle-making."

He grinned, put his hands up in surrender. "I admit defeat."

"Good," she snapped, backing up so she could pull out of the driveway.

"Tomorrow?" he called. "Magical mastery is happening tomorrow?"

She snorted and shifted into drive. "Yes. I get off at six. Come by at seven. I'll make you dinner."

He nodded. "Oh, Tilly?" he asked as she began to creep forward.

She braked, hand on the window crank. "Yeah?"

"I took that ride because you offered," he said, coming close enough to rest his hands on the top of her car, voice rasping, words quiet but no less powerful because of it. "Because you're beautiful and interesting . . ."

Her breath caught.

"And because I can't seem to stay away from you."

She knew the feeling. *God,* did she know the feeling.

It was a miracle she didn't hit anything on the way home.

But it *wasn't* a miracle to see Rex's car pause at the bottom of her driveway, for her to peek through her curtains and wave at him before he drove off, for the text to make her phone buzz.

My favorite flowers are hydrangeas. My mom loved them.

Her heart pounded as she typed back a response. Those things weren't miracles, Rex checking up on her, following her home, texting her before bed . . . none of them were a surprise.

For some insane reason, she'd begun to expect those actions from Rex.

And that was what scared her the most.

FIFTEEN

Rex

HE PULLED up the driveway to Tilly's house, parked, then walked straight across her front porch. There would be no hiding in the bushes any longer.

Nope.

Rex had decided to put his impulsivity to the test, stop over-thinking everything, and to just go with it. Not that he had a snowball's chance in hell in staying away from her anyway.

She whipped open the door, ponytail askew, cheeks flushed red, and still in her diner uniform. "You're early."

The door slammed closed.

"Um."

He knocked again, but the only thing he got in response was another, "You're early," though it was significantly more muffled and trailed by the sound of footsteps. But instead of those steps coming back toward the door, instead of Tilly opening it and letting him in, they moved away.

Rex waited a minute, listening intently. There were more footfalls, a crash or two, and then after a long moment, nothing.

He hesitated, trying to track her movements again, but when after a few more heartbeats, he still heard nothing, Rex tried the knob. It turned, and he pushed the door open, slipping into the house.

Small, was his first thought, but not in a negative way in the least. Her living room held a love seat, coffee table, and bookcase, and while none of the furniture matched and there were more than a few dings, scratches, and worn spots, the whole effect was cozy and comfortable. Not decorated by a designer to be magazine-worthy, to capture that false sense of country chic, but real life.

Lived in rather than put on a shelf.

And everything smelled fucking incredible—cinnamon and earthy with just the hint of something floral that made his mind want to go in and check it out

He turned to study the kitchen but didn't get further than identifying it as the source of the lovely smell and seeing the counter stacked with a variety of bowls and other vessels before he heard a loud *thunk* followed by a pained cry.

Moving before his brain finished processing the noise, he sprinted down the hall, passed an open door leading to the bathroom then burst into Tilly's bedroom. How did he know that it was her bedroom? Well, smart man that he was, Rex was able to deduce it was the place she slept because there was a bed in the middle of the room. Congratulate him now, Alec.

His eyes didn't stay on the bed for long, however. Because while he'd spent the last few days imagining what it might be like to get Tilly into a bed, the sight actually in front of him was much more tempting than a mattress and silk sheets.

What?

A man had to dream, didn't he?

But for now, he had to focus . . . on committing every single one of the details in front of him to memory.

Because Tilly was in her bedroom. Topless.

Fucking gorgeous, tits bouncing as she struggled to get out of her shirt. He couldn't figure out how she'd managed to get stuck, the tangle of bra and cotton completely covering her face, while her arms were somehow bound straight over her head.

Perfect nipples. Deliciously curved waist. Hips that he wanted to—

She yanked at the shirt, a pathetic mewl escaping her lips before transforming into another pained cry as she crashed into the dresser along one side of the room.

Fuck.

He was standing there ogling her, and she was hurt.

Ass.

But that didn't stop him from staring at her for a few moments longer. Fuck, she had perfect breasts. Rex swallowed, tore his eyes from her chest, and affected a casual, "Need a hand?"

She shrieked, making him jump. "Don't look!" she shouted, turning her back on him and managing to catch herself on the corner of the dresser. He caught her before her head collided with the sharp corner. "Don't you dare look, Rex Roosevelt."

"Not a chance in hell, sweetheart," he said, studying the mess that was the tangle of her bra and shirt. "Not a chance in hell of ignoring the most perfect pair of breasts I've ever seen." His fingers lifted, started working at the knot, and he fucking deserved a medal for doing that rather than drifting them lower, stroking over the hardened buds of her nipples, or better yet, sucking one deep into his mouth.

Tilly's sigh was outraged, and she tried to slip away from him. "You're a pig."

"Yep." A beat. "Now hold still. I think I see where you're caught."

"It's my hair," she groaned.

"That and the hook on the back of your bra. Let me just . . . *there.*" He managed to release the tiny hook from the T-shirt then set to work on unwrapping the strands of gold silk. "How'd you get stuck?"

If those hazel eyes had been on his, if the cotton was out of the way, Rex had no doubt they'd have been narrowed into a glare. "Because you were *early.*"

"Why are you saying that like it's a bad thing?"

She huffed as he worked on the final knot of hair. "Because I was late getting off work and still trying to get set up, and you showed up *early.*"

"So, it's my fault because you were late?"

"Yes." Another sigh. "No. I just wanted to get out of these clothes and wash my face. I smell like the diner."

He sniffed. "I love the way you smell." Tilly froze, but Rex kept working on the tangle until . . . *there.* She was free at last. He tugged the shirt up and over her head then placed it in front of her chest before she could so much as blink.

"I—" She clutched the cotton to her breasts then sighed, defeat creeping into her expression. "Why do I always seem to be thanking you?"

He didn't like the direction of her thoughts in the least, so he waggled his brows, a teasing smile on his lips. "If you keep letting me see your tits, you can forgo the *thank yous.*" Pink had already stained her cheeks, but his words made them go even brighter, and his dick twitched in response. Naked breasts, fiery eyes, and pink cheeks . . . fucking slayed him.

"Pig," she accused, smacking his chest. However, in doing so, she managed to lose her grip on the shirt and it fell to the floor.

Rex wasn't a fucking gentleman, so he didn't pick it up. He also sure as shit let his gaze drift back down. *Fucking hell.* "You're welcome," he said, mouth curving, still not helping her as she fought to scoop up the cotton for a few moments then attempted to situate it over those luscious curves.

"I wasn't thanking you," she grumbled.

"I know. But my mom instilled a manner or two in this lascivious mind." He tapped his temple, grinned, and turned to leave. "Get dressed. I'll meet you in the kitchen."

"Rex?"

He stopped in the doorway, turned back.

Tilly crossed over to him. "Why were you early?"

He was tempted to lie, to make up some excuse about just hating to be late or running ahead of schedule, but he found that with her eyes on his, Rex *couldn't* lie to her.

"Why?" she pressed when he didn't immediately reply.

"I needed to see you," he said softly.

"Oh." She was close enough that he felt the heat of her breath on his lips. "I was hoping you would say that."

"I—"

But the rest of his sentence was lost because instead of her breath on his lips, suddenly the shirt was gone, her fingers were woven into his hair, and her mouth was on his.

Fuck, her mouth was on his.

And it was *everything*.

SIXTEEN

Tilly

OKAY, so launching herself topless at Rex Roosevelt may not have been the best idea, she realized. But it was too late. She'd leaped, and now she was topless and in Rex's arms because he'd caught her reflexively. But that was it.

He'd caught her. She'd kissed him.

Then hadn't moved.

Not one muscle.

Cheeks burning, mortification tearing down her spine, Tilly started to pull back.

"I'm—"

She'd been about to say she was sorry, but the words didn't emerge because her mouth had suddenly become otherwise occupied.

By Rex's.

His tongue thrust through her parted lips and swept inside, rubbing against hers in a rhythm that had her squirming close. Especially when his hands drifted up her sides, roughened fingertips brushing along the outside of her breasts.

Fuck yeah, that was good.

She arched, shifting and squirming until his palm shifted over, squeezing her, fingers now teasing her nipples.

And . . . nirvana.

He pulled back and she swayed on her feet, head spinning, not fully cognizant that her oxygen had been so limited. Thus was the power of Rex Roosevelt. One kiss and she got stupid . . . or passed out from a lack of fresh air.

But he tasted like mint and cinnamon, and they both knew how she felt about cinnamon. Spicy, intoxicating—

Any hope of a lucid thought flew out of her head. Rex's mouth moved from hers, drifted along her jaw. He nipped at her earlobe, making gooseflesh break out all over her body and slid lower, kissing down her throat, teeth grazing her collarbone.

Then lower still.

"Oh, God," she moaned when he latched onto her nipple, sucking it deeply as he pinched and rolled her neglected side between his thumb and forefinger.

Desire arrowed through her, spreading through her limbs, making her lips tingle and her thighs press together. Her panties were absolutely soaked, and she wanted nothing more than to strip off her jeans, climb on top of Rex, then take them both for a wild ride. As though reading her mind, he slid his palms down her torso, flicked open the button of her jeans and shoved them down to her knees. But instead of scooping her up and tossing her on the bed as she'd imagined, he leaned in and pressed his mouth to her.

Hot breath through thin cotton.

Damp heat against her pussy.

Her eyes rolled back and before she could think about what he was doing or the fact that she'd worked a full shift and hadn't showered, her underwear joined her jeans and his tongue was on her clit.

"*Oh fuck,*" she said, knees buckling.

Rex guided her down to the rug, yanking off her clothes and shoving his shoulders between her thighs.

And then he got to work.

Glorious, incredible work.

Spreading her wide with one hand, he circled the flat of his tongue around her clit, then slid one finger of the other hand inside, pumping slow and steady and deep. Tilly cried out, hips arching, wanting him closer, wanting more, wanting—

"Rex," she groaned when he added another finger and timed their motion to that of his tongue. Fire pumped through her veins, scorching her limbs, coalescing in her center, coiling tighter and tighter and tighter until finally it exploded outward. She cried out, pleasure coursing through her, lids slamming shut, and when she finally managed to open them, what felt like hours later, Tilly was half-surprised that her body hadn't been reduced to ash.

That orgasm had been—

Holy fuck is what it'd been.

Rex shifted, and she felt a bolt of embarrassment shoot through her when she realized he was still between her thighs, chin glistening, blue eyes molten.

She bit her lip. "I—um—" Clenching her teeth together, she cut off the words, just barely able to stop herself from asking if she'd tasted okay. A little late for that *now.*

He lifted the hem of his shirt and wiped his mouth. "What?"

"That was incredible," she murmured.

A smirk. "Yes, it was," he said and crawled up her body, still fully dressed. He slipped an arm under her shoulders, tugged her against his chest. "But that also wasn't what you were going to say."

Her jaw dropped open. "How do you always know?"

"Because for whatever reason, the universe has decided to throw us together," he said. "And for as different as our lives have been up until this point, I don't think either of us can deny that we have a connection that can only come from shared experiences."

She scoffed.

"Okay, how about similar experiences?" he asked. "Because I have the feeling you know exactly what it feels like to be on the outside looking in."

"I—" She broke off, shock coursing through her. He was right. That—her role as the perpetual outsider—had been her entire childhood. It didn't matter if she was at school or at home, but she'd never felt like she had a place, and eventually she'd begun to keep people at a distance to stop herself from feeling that way.

So much easier, so much *safer* that way.

He brushed back her hair from her forehead. "I see you know exactly what I mean."

She nodded. "I do. I—" She broke off again.

Another strand of hair tucked safely behind her ear. "No?" he asked, when she didn't finish her thought for the second time.

"No," she agreed.

"Hmm." He nuzzled her throat, and she shivered when his voice rumbled against her skin. "So, perhaps we should circle back to the first conversation? To what you stopped yourself from saying?"

"Um . . ."

"No?" he asked again when she trailed off. "Well, I guess I'll fill in the blanks for you then." His mouth found her ear. "You tasted fucking incredible, baby. Sweet like that cinnamon roll with the barest hint of spicy tartness. It was the absolute best meal of my life."

Her pulse pounded, the words colliding with a spot deep

within her heart.

But instead of harming her, of knocking a piece of herself loose, of bruising or slicing, they bolstered . . . and frankly, they turned her on.

Turned her into a smoldering pile of mush.

Or maybe just her brain because when he asked, "Who made you feel like you were on the outside, baby?" she actually answered.

"My mother," she said softly. "My father." A long slow breath. "And my fiancé."

"You're engaged?" Rex stiffened, drawing his arm out from beneath her so quickly that her head *thunked* against the floor. Thank God for the thick rug.

Blinking, she sat up, crossed her arms over her chest, suddenly vulnerable and self-conscious. "Was," she said. "*Was* engaged."

"Oh." He sat up, stripping off his shirt and slipping it over her head.

Even though she had a perfectly good drawer full of shirts, she let him. Hell, more than let him. Tilly curled into the warm cotton, drew in a lungful of his spicy scent, crisscrossing her legs so it covered her from shoulders to toes.

"He broke up with me not long after my mom passed."

"Asshole."

Her mouth turned up. "Yes. Yes, he was."

"What happened?"

"To my mom? Or with Steven?"

"Both."

She didn't think she could handle this conversation, naked except for a T-shirt, on her bedroom floor. She needed armor, barriers between her and the past. And this room with its memories of her mother, of her time with Steven . . . it was too much.

"I need to put on pants for this," she muttered. "And maybe a bra."

"Shame that," Rex said lightly, but he stood and crossed to her dresser, opening the top drawer and holding up one of her most-worn sports bras. From the next drawer, he extracted her favorite pair of pajamas, lilac and covered with unicorns. They were threadbare and ready to split at the seams, but they were also so freaking cozy that she couldn't bear to part with them. He seemed to study the waistband for a moment and Tilly wondered if he were checking the size.

Seemed a little nosy if anyone asked her.

But also . . . he'd been nose-deep in her vagina only minutes before, so it wasn't like she had room to be outraged.

He knelt and slipped them over her feet, helped her slide them up to her hips then handed her the sports bra. "Have any alcohol in that kitchen of yours?" he asked. "Seems like you might need it."

Considering the mere thought of her parents and Steven had driven her to drink many times before, Tilly couldn't fault his logic.

"Vodka in the freezer. Sprite and orange juice in the fridge."

"Screwdriver on steroids," he said. "I like it." A kiss to the top of her head. "I'll make yours a double."

"Why?" she asked as he started to walk from the room. "Why are you here?"

What could you possibly see in me?

That was the question running through her head.

And once again, he seemed to be able to read her mind.

He closed the distance between them and kissed her fiercely, one hand cupping her cheek, the other squeezing her hip. "You," he murmured when he broke free. "I see *you*."

He paused in the doorway.

"And that's enough."

SEVENTEEN

Rex

HIS BODY RADIATED with tension as he strode down the hall and into the kitchen.

Only part of it was sexual because his cock was still rock-hard and throbbing. But he barely focused on that as he pulled out the bottle of vodka from the freezer, along with the Sprite and orange juice from the fridge, and *that* was saying something. Rex wasn't the kind of man to forgo his own sexual urges in place of conversation, and he *definitely* wasn't a man who was jealous over an asshole from a woman's past.

Probably because *he* usually was the asshole from the past.

Snorting, he searched the cabinets until he located two glasses and then fixed them both strong drinks. Because the rest of his tension had been strongly from anticipation . . . or maybe dread.

Anticipation because he wanted to know everything about Tilly—the secrets and long-buried hurts, her hopes and dreams for the future.

Dread because he knew that if he wanted to have a snow-ball's chance in hell of that future possibly including him, then he would need to level with her about his past in the very same way.

Talking and sharing feelings were almost as scary words to him as responsibility.

And yet here he was. Not running but digging in and preparing to stay.

To fight to stay.

Rex couldn't deny that was one feeling he actually enjoyed.

Footsteps and creaking floorboards announced Tilly's arrival before she walked tentatively around the corner and into the kitchen. Eyes landing on the glasses but not on him, she all but snatched one from his hand and downed the contents.

"Um. Okay?" he asked.

She nodded, took his glass and started chugging.

"I don't think—"

"I do," she said. "Because if I'm going to tell you about my parents and Steven, then I need alcohol in my life."

"Well, then." He refilled and held out her glass.

She took it, gulped. Then, cheeks pinkened, though this time not for a reason he viewed as particularly pleasant, Tilly lifted her chin and said, "My mom blamed me for my dad leaving."

His brows drew together. "What? No—" he began.

"I'm not telling you this as some sort of emotional reasoning or baggage or hurt feelings a kid holds on to." She put both glasses in the sink then began returning the bottles to their respective locations. "I'm saying this as an adult woman who is fully aware of her parents' opinions because she *lived* them." A beat. "And also because she told me in no uncertain terms."

Shadows in those hazel depths. "The first time I remember

her telling me that was as my dad drove down the driveway before he left us the first time. A dust cloud trailed him, lingering in the air for far longer than his car."

"How old were you?"

"Six? Seven?" she said. "Young enough to not understand what he was doing and too old not to miss him once he'd gone."

"Why did he leave?"

She leaned back against the counter. "I wasn't exactly an easy child. I was a preemie and didn't sleep much at all for the first two years. And I was energetic, needy. I couldn't entertain myself, had to have an adult keep me occupied or I got in trouble."

He frowned. "So you were a normal six or seven-year-old kid."

"I guess."

The silence stretched for a few moments before Rex asked, "You said the first time he left?"

"Oh, yeah." Tilly smiled, but it wasn't a happy one. "My parents were special. They couldn't stay together, couldn't live apart. They were like the most fucked-up drug addicts, but their relationship was their drug of choice." She sighed. "Unfortunately, even though they couldn't stay away from each other for long, they also couldn't make each other happy."

"And you were stuck in the crossfire."

"Happily so," she said, surprising him. Then added, no doubt at his confused look, "It was attention, and I was starving for it."

His heart skipped a beat, and her eyes softened as she took in his face. He was still shirtless and when she placed her hand over his heart, the soft skin of her palm made goose bumps break out on his skin. "You know something about that, don't you?" she murmured. "Know what it's like to feel so lonely and isolated that you'll take any form of attention."

He nodded, sucked in a breath, and just laid his cards on the table. "I was the bad twin, never as smart or talented as Justin, so I stopped trying, and eventually, I learned to love the negative attention, took pleasure in their shock and disappointment."

"Better a disappointment than ignored."

Rex brushed his fingers over her cheek. "Yes. That."

"But it's not healthy."

He shook his head. "No."

"And when I was ten, my dad left for good." Her lips pressed flat for a long moment. "I thought it would only be a matter of time before he came back. It wasn't like that was the first time he'd disappeared for a few weeks to cool off." She swallowed hard, pulled out the vodka bottle and splashed some more in her glass. "I remember getting home from school every day and rushing into their bedroom"—she pointed down the hall —"but he was never there. Then I'd stand here in the kitchen and watch through the window until he came home."

"But he didn't come back?"

"No."

For some reason, the image of ten-year-old Tilly staring through the small window, watching the street for any sign of her father's car coming up the driveway sliced him to the core. Okay, not for *some* reason, because he wasn't a monster and didn't want to see any kid hurt, emotionally or otherwise.

But it hit him harder than normal because it was Tilly.

And he could picture it.

And he wanted to pummel anyone who'd ever so much as hurt her feelings.

"So—" He stopped, shoving the question of what she'd done after her father had gone deep down. They'd drudged up enough tonight and—

"We stayed in this house," she murmured. "On pause for ages. Waiting for him to show back up, waiting for our lives to start again. I think that's why I got into scents so much. I found an old bottle of my dad's cologne and tried to replicate it." Her smile was sad. "I think part of me thought that if I could just make the house smell like him again, then maybe . . . oh God, it's so stupid now."

"You hoped he might come back."

She rolled her eyes. "Unfortunately, yes."

"Shit, baby," he said and took her in his arms. Rex had rarely comforted another person. It wasn't his instinct or nature or . . . style, he supposed, to focus on someone who wasn't himself. Or maybe he'd been so closed down that he hadn't been able to recognize when someone might need something from him.

He definitely hadn't been capable of giving it.

But over the last few years, things had begun shifting. He'd seen his brother and Kelly happy and hadn't acted selfishly for once. He'd helped Bella. And he wanted to do the same thing for Tilly.

No. He wanted to do more.

"It was stupid," she said, burrowing into his chest with a sniff. "To stop living for so long. But after a month had passed then two then more, my mom just sort of shut down, I guess. She stopped picking me up from school, and I started walking home. She didn't cook dinner or buy groceries."

"How did you live?"

"My dad sent money," she said softly. "Enough for me to stretch after my mom stopped showing up for work and lost her job." She shoved out of his arms. "This town never got it. They thought she was lazy, that she was just after a free ride." Tilly paced away. "They didn't understand she was depressed, that she literally could *not* get out of bed. I was fine. I cashed the checks, bought food, cooked."

He snagged her hand as she paced by, tugging her against him, and this time she stayed in the circle of his arms. "Henry's mom and dad were the only ones who understood. They never gave me those judgy looks and when I was old enough, I got a job at the diner."

"How old was old enough?"

She smiled. "Fourteen. Not legal, I know," she added. "But he paid me in food, and it was so much better than anything I could cook up at the time that it was like I'd brought home food from a four-star Michelin chef. My mom even perked up for a time."

"Why do I sense a *but* coming?"

Tilly sighed. "Probably because there is one."

"I was afraid of that."

A shrug. "It's not that unusual. She got sick. Things got even tighter. I made it work . . . and then she died."

"How old were you?"

"Seventeen." She straightened her shoulders, tried to pull away again, but he wouldn't let her. No distance between them. Not in this moment. "Luckily, I was only two months shy of eighteen, so by the time they figured out I was a minor, I was legal."

"But you were alone."

"I got used to being alone long before my mother passed."

Silence stretched between them for a long moment, and Rex would be lying if he'd said he knew how to comfort her. The pain in her words had been acute, but it was also an old hurt, and he thought that harping on it might make things worse. And then there was the fact that she'd now bared her soul, and he probably needed to reciprocate and—

Cool fingers cupped his jaw.

"Too much?" she asked.

Rex slipped his hand behind her neck, held her in place when her gaze would have drifted away from his. "No," he said.

"I was just thinking that this meant I needed to tell you every-thing about my childhood, too, and—"

"It's a lot?"

"Nothing when compared to what you went through, which makes me a giant asshole because I spent so many years acting like—" He sighed. "And you were dealing with all this— And I wasted so much fucking time just being—"

She placed a finger over his lips. "There's a lot happening here, but I think the first thing you need to do is finish a sentence." Her mouth curved. "And know that just because I told you a bunch of shit about my past doesn't mean you have to reciprocate in turn tonight."

He pressed a kiss to her finger then lifted it from his face. "But—"

"Shh," she said and rose on tiptoe to slant her lips across his. Then she dropped back down to the balls of her feet. "Enough," she said. "For tonight, let's just let this be enough."

He hesitated, warring with himself, knowing he should share but fucking terrified to put himself out there. It was easy to fix a car or to buy a phone. Emotions, on the other hand? Scary as shit. But as he watched Tilly, her eyes soft and kind, no trace of disappointment or anger in her expression, he thought that perhaps they weren't so scary after all. Though, it wasn't a thought with one hundred percent certainty, because when she laced her fingers with his and tugged him over to one of the many bowls on the counter, waxing poetic about the scent she'd come up with for his cinnamon roll candle, he didn't put the activity on pause.

Instead, he went along for the ride.

He let himself enjoy the process, soaked up Tilly and spending time with a woman because she was fun and smart and witty.

Soon he'd have to lay it all out there.

But tonight, he'd just take this moment.

And for the first time in his life, instead of throwing it away or treating it as casual and unimportant, Rex clutched it tight, tucked it safe inside his heart.

Where Tilly had already made a permanent place for herself.

EIGHTEEN

Tilly

SHE TAUGHT Rex how to make cinnamon roll scented candles and then he helped her fill her outstanding orders that had come in with sudden, shocking frequency.

"I don't know how she got my name," Tilly said, holding up the paper with the information. "I don't think I ever met her at the couple of craft fairs I go to, and yet she's ordered six dozen toiletry sets. But," she added with a smile, "if this keeps up, I might finally be able to open up my own place."

"Seems to me, it's finally your time to shine," Rex said, tongue poking out in rather adorable fashion as he filled lip balm tubes with her lemon-raspberry concoction.

Maybe it was the way he said it or perhaps it was knowing that he'd been behind her car and her phone, that finally a niggle of something penetrated her thoughts. "Please, don't tell me you have a warehouse of my candles and shampoos somewhere."

"What?" He jerked, overflowing several of the tubes, and glancing up at her with a definitely guilty expression.

"Oh, my God," she moaned. "You do."

She clanked the spoon on the counter, turned off the heat on the wax she was melting, tears filling her eyes, and mortification burning through her. The phone, the car, and now he'd bought close to ten thousand dollars in candles?

Well, candles, shampoos, face wash, lip balm—

Not the point, Conner.

She should have known this wasn't something she'd done on her own. This was another fucking handout.

Rex might like her, might *want* her in bed, but he was just like everyone else. He didn't think she was a fully capable human being, didn't think she could make things work on her own, even though she'd always managed, had clawed and squeaked through tight spots more times in her life than anyone ever should have.

She'd told him everything . . . and he was just the same as everyone else.

Not fair, her brain cautioned her, but it was too little too late. Her temper had sparked, and she was vulnerable and embarrassed and—

"Get out," she snapped, brushing by him and picking up her laptop.

"What are you doing?"

"Canceling the fucking orders," she gritted out. "Refunding your money. I can't believe you'd buy—"

"Why wouldn't I buy it?" he asked. "It's fucking incredible. But I—"

"I told you to leave," she said. "I can't believe I was stupid enough to think that things would be different, that I would finally get out of debt. Or worse, that someone might actually think I could be a fully capable person all on my own."

Rex closed her laptop before she could actually cancel anything. "You are!"

She growled, tried to open it again, but he didn't let her. Instead, he snatched up the computer and shoved it on top of the fridge. And because she was a short motherfucker, she couldn't reach it without getting a stool.

Which she did. Snatching it from the pantry and plunking it down in front of the fridge.

Tilly clambered up, reached on tiptoe and—

Nearly fell.

Nearly because Rex caught her and set her firmly on the floor.

"I don't need a rescue!" she screamed, shoving away from him and trying to sprint from the room. "Just go," she spat, when he snagged her arm to stop her. "Go, like all the rest of them and save me the heartache later."

Rex froze, not speaking for a long moment, then he cursed, yanked her against his chest and wrapped his arms around her in a hug she really wanted to pretend she didn't want.

"What is it, exactly, that has you so upset?"

Tilly huffed, tried to squirm free of his hold.

"You're such a fucking asshole." She glared up at him when he held firm.

"That we all know." One brow came up. "So, care to share?"

"No," she muttered, feeling extremely childish and still not willing to give in.

"Fine," he said and tossed her onto his shoulder. He spent a moment at the stove, and though she couldn't see him since she was getting an eyeful of an attractive ass she didn't want to admit she was staring at, she still heard the *click* of the knobs, the slight whoosh of the gas turning off. "Will they be okay?"

She knew he was referring to the scents she had steeping and while part of her wanted to be touched by his kindness— and all the other kindnesses he'd shown her over the last days— the rest of her was seriously pissed off.

Maybe unreasonably so, but still fucking furious.

"They'll be fine," she snapped. "And I will, too, once you let me down and get the hell out of my house."

"Good."

But he didn't put her down, and he didn't walk out the front door. Instead, he carried her down the hall into her bedroom, dropped her onto the mattress, then crawled in beside her.

Yeah, not happening.

She started to get up, but Rex caught her waist, pulled her against him, and . . . just held her.

Held her.

His hand didn't move up or down to cop a feel, he didn't thrust his crotch against her ass. He didn't try to kiss her or talk dirty or get her naked. He. Just. Held. Her.

Until she stopped fighting.

Until she slowly relaxed against him.

Until her anger peaked and began decreasing infinitesimally.

Only then did he speak. "I don't have a warehouse of your products. I called a few friends, suggested they check out your stuff. *They* decided to order it. They paid for it." She felt him shrug. "I merely suggested it."

Tilly shifted in the circle of his arms, rolling to face him, to see his eyes. "You're not lying."

He shook his head. "I'm not."

"You . . . suggested?"

"Yes." His gaze stayed on hers, but she could read between the lines.

A snort. "I'm guessing you *strongly* suggested."

Blue eyes rolled. "I'm a Roosevelt. All of our *suggestions* are strong."

"Really?"

He smirked. "Should I add large as well?"

Tilly laughed, but it wasn't entirely comfortable. She was feeling a bit stupid for having overreacted the way she had, especially when he'd been nothing but nice and fun and had given her the best orgasm of her life. The memory of that mouth on her, his tongue flicking against her clit was enough for her cheeks to heat, her thighs to clench.

His thumb brushed over her skin. "Is this from my bad innuendos?"

"No." She sucked in a breath then stifled a moan when she got a whiff of his delicious scent.

"Hmm?" He cupped her jaw, bent to nuzzle her throat. "Then what?"

"Your cock," she blurted. "I was thinking about your mouth on me and how that was fucking incredible and how you'd probably feel even better inside me—"

He froze, pulled back. "Sweetheart, you can't say things like that."

Tilly smiled and cupped his cheek with her palm. "I'm sorry."

"For making my dick hard or for freaking out earlier?"

"Well, definitely not the first." She smiled when he groaned and flopped to his back. "What?" She climbed on top of him, straddling his hips. "I find that I'm rather fine with making this"—a shift of her hips—"hard."

"Fine?" His hands came to her waist. "Just *fine?*"

"Is adequate better? Perhaps satisfying?"

He growled. "Woman, you have to be the most infuriating creature on the planet."

Stilling, the smile dropping from her lips, she stared down at the beautiful man beneath her. "I really am sorry. I tend not to lose my temper, but when I do, I admit that I go a bit overboard. And this wasn't even really about you so much as it was about Steven."

"We'll circle back to that asshole, Steven part," he said, leaning up and pressing a hard kiss to her lips. "Because I like your temper, baby. I don't mind you getting fired up or upset or angry. I just want you to be you. And more than that, I always want you to feel like you can be you with me." He tugged the end of her ponytail. "Even if you think I won't like it. Okay?"

She nodded.

"Now, Steven?"

"It's a small thing, really. No, I don't mean the way it made me feel," she said, hurrying to add when Rex's eyes narrowed and his mouth opened, no doubt to protest her statement. Fair that, since what she was calling a *small thing* had caused such a big reaction. "Because it did make me feel shitty, but more because I didn't realize how much it had upset me until everything hit me in the kitchen."

He touched her cheek. "I want to be following, sweetheart, but I'm a little confused. It seems like a big thing because you had a huge reaction, but you're telling me it's not important."

She plunked her forehead to his chest. "I . . . okay, I guess this is so hard because I thought I was over Steven completely. We were young when we were engaged, and I thought he was my white knight put on the planet to rescue me." She rolled her eyes. "Stupid, I know. But I think I wanted it to be true for so long that I just . . . let it be that way." Ripping out her ponytail holder, she sighed. "Is this making any sense at all? I mean, I thought Steven would swoop in and fill all the empty holes in me, and he was really good at taking care of me. I think he even liked it. The saving part made him feel good."

"But?"

"But at some point, he resented it," she said. "And I get it. I wasn't even eighteen yet, he was barely twenty, commuting to school during the week, seeing me on the weekends. I was a wreck and had no clue what to do and—" A sigh. "Eventually, he couldn't take it anymore, couldn't take how sad I was, how I sometimes forgot to eat or struggled with filling out insurance papers because I didn't want to put pen to paper and admit she was gone. I was depressed and unable, unwilling, to find help and . . . something gave. He left." She sucked in a breath. "I went into a tailspin, didn't get out of bed for a week, didn't eat, didn't sleep. I was heartbroken and alone, but one day it was like the fog cleared. I realized that if I was ever going to get out of this town, then I had to figure my own shit out." A beat. "By myself. Without a man to—"

"So, you think because I fixed your car and got you a phone, because I mentioned—"

"Strongly suggested," she interrupted with a raised brow.

He smirked. "Because I suggested to a friend that she try out your products and maybe roll them out to a few boutique hotels, that I'm going to get resentful of you?"

"I'm—" She started to deny it, but then realized, yes, that was exactly what she was afraid of.

He'd find out about the bills and pay them off.

Her car would break down, and he'd buy her a new one.

Her roof would collapse, and then she'd come home to find it fixed.

He'd swoop in and do the saving, and what could she possibly give in return to him?

Nothing.

Because she *had* nothing, couldn't compete with the Roosevelt wealth or power. She was just a twenty-six-year-old girl trying to figure shit out, had spent the last eight years trying to sort out her shit so she could move on to bigger and better things, and he wouldn't see any of that if he just swept into her life, snapped his fingers, and made everything perfect.

And so, she told him that.

"Rex, you're *you*. Your family is powerful. You're rich, and I know you can fix things in my life that are nearly impossible for me to even dream about mending easily."

"But you don't want that." He seemed genuinely confused, poor thing.

"No," she murmured with a smile. "I don't want a partner who needs to save me all the time."

He tucked a strand of her hair behind her ear. "But isn't that what real relationships are all about? You save each other."

"Each other, I think, are the keys words there. Because Rex, what can I possibly hope to do for you? I can't compete with the money or the influence." Her gaze drifted to the floor, to the spot that had rotted away. She'd repaired it with plywood, thrown a rug over the top, and no one was the wiser.

Except her.

She was the wiser and just like the floor, she was just a patchwork of mismatched pieces, cobbled together to make some semblance of a whole.

How could she possibly be an equal partner with anyone if she could barely keep her head above water?

"Come here."

Her gaze jumped back to his. "What?"

"Come here," he murmured, tugging her back to his chest and covering them both with a blanket. "Let me tell you a story, darling."

"Darling?" She snorted. "And a story?" She clapped her hands together. "Oh my God! Really?"

Fingers on her cheek. "There's my sarcastic girl."

"And you like sarcasm?"

"I like you. So fucking much, sweetheart." His fingers tightened on her arm, not painful, but strong with intention, exactly like the words that followed. "I spent so much of my life in a fog, flitting from one thing to the next, trying to feel something after my mom died. You see?" he said, when her eyes filled with tears.

"Instead of doing something important, like trying to build a life for myself, after my mother died, I just shut down. I lived to numb every feeling, pushed everyone away. And . . . I hurt so many people who mattered."

"You were hurting."

"Yes," he agreed. "But I was also an asshole. I know I lost my mom and that my dad retreated into himself for way too long, especially considering that he had Justin and myself to raise, but I chose the wrong path."

"You were young and—"

"No more excuses for me, sweetheart." He smiled at her, a gentle, fragile thing. "They're all true, but what's also true is that I walked, drove like a crazy fucker in one of my ridiculous sports cars down that path for way too long." She laughed, and he wiped the corner of her eye, where a tear had gathered. "Then, I met Kelly."

He paused and the smile she was wearing slipped away.

Because he'd said—

Kelly.

And not her.

Oh God, was he still hung up on her?

"No," he said gently. "It's not her I want. What I was trying to say is I met her, saw her with my brother, and I realized how different things could be. They took a tragedy and tough situation and turned it into something unbreakable."

Tilly's heart settled.

"Then Bella thought I was my brother in Italy and the way she looked at me with such hope—no, not *hope*, exactly, but conviction. Like she knew that Justin would do the right thing. That without one iota of doubt, he'd help her . . . and then I saw the way it faded when she realized I was me." He rolled his eyes at himself. "My ego was bruised, but more than that, I saw in that moment I had the opportunity to change."

"And you did."

He scoffed. "I'm at least trying."

"Well, coming from a stranger you helped on the side of the road, I can vouch for that change."

He brushed a kiss on her forehead. "That wasn't selfless in the least. I saw a beautiful *angel* through the window and had to stop."

"Have X-ray vision, do you?" she teased. "Being able to see into a car in the dead of night." She ran her hands over his chest, stopped at the space above his heart. "You stopped because this is good inside."

"Maybe," he said.

"And the universe rewarded you with me." She chuckled. "A mess of a project with more baggage than the belly of a plane."

"Baggage, I'm happy to help carry, sweetheart."

Her lips curved. "Only if you'll let me carry yours, too."

"Deal, Angel," he said, his eyes dancing. "Deal."

A sigh before she hugged him tight. "I let you get away with the first *Angel,* but I can't let that second one slide."

He laughed, cuddling her closer when she yawned. "Sleep now. We can negotiate tomorrow."

Burrowing into his arms, she soaked in his scent. "You always smell too good."

"So, turn me into a candle then."

Exhaustion swept over her, the emotions of the evening and the late hour catching up with her, but she laughed at his joke, though that laugh transmuted into another yawn.

"Sleep now," he murmured. "We can argue more in the morning."

NINETEEN

Rex

"ARE you sure you can't come?" he asked a few days later, standing near the hostess stand of Henry's Diner, box filled with Bella's delicious baked goods in one hand and Tilly's ass in the other.

Speaking of that, he shifted his hand upward. It was late, so the diner crowd was decidedly older, but they were garnering a fair amount of attention, and he didn't want to scar the odd child that was in the restaurant. Especially when he'd been trying to just give his girl a simple kiss goodbye, and as things were wont to do with Tilly, they'd heated up and almost gotten out of hand.

Pun intended.

He snorted inwardly and placed his hand determinedly on the small of her back.

Reddened lips tipping up at the corners, Tilly brushed one more kiss across his cheek. "Trying to be good, Roosevelt?"

"Attempting to, yes."

She rose on tiptoe, whispered in his ear. "I like you a little bad."

He groaned softly and turned to glare at her. "You're not helping."

"Have a little problem?" She smirked.

"I resent the term *little*," he muttered, releasing her and stepping back, strategically placing the box of baked goods in front of his groin.

"And, yes," she said, regret rather than teasing in her words. "I'm sorry, I can't join you for dinner, but with Sally calling out, I don't want to leave Henry shorthanded."

"I understand. Call me when you're off?"

She nodded, and he turned to go.

"Rex?"

He paused, slanting a look over his shoulder and lifting a brow.

"You know that *this*"—she pointed between them—"will reach Kel and Justin before you do?"

Considering that Esther, the head gossip in town, had her phone out and was recording them, Rex very much knew that. He blew a kiss at Tilly, chuckling when Esther cackled something about great material for Snapchat. "Meh."

"Really?" she asked. "You're that cavalier about this? About everyone talking about what's going on with us?"

He spun to face her, stole one more kiss. "Cavalier?" he said, breaking away once they were both breathing hard. "Not in the least. You're mine, and I'm counting on the gossip train to inform everyone of that fact, sweetheart." He started for the door. "Because I don't share well."

"Rex!"

He turned his head and met her stare.

"Just for the record," she said, eyes hot. "I don't share well either."

He was smiling the entire drive to Kelly and Justin's.

Yeah, he'd most definitely met his match.

HIS BROTHER HAD BEEN SLANTING him looks across the dinner table the entire evening.

Kelly had cooked—or rather, she'd heated up a dish that her sister, Melissa, had left earlier that afternoon as a thanks for riding lessons—and they were all chowing down. If not for the looks, Rex would have been relaxed—the kids were eating happily, no plates had hit the floor, and no arguments had broken out.

But Justin kept staring at him, not saying anything, acting completely normal with the rest of the table, and yet with him . . .

Weird.

Rex sighed. Because not *weird*, exactly. He could sense the impending conversation and had been a fucking moron for not recognizing that it would be coming. Justin was worried about Tilly.

And Rex couldn't stop himself from thinking that his brother was right to worry.

Fuck.

They'd all just about finished when there was a knock at the door. He remembered a time when he would have heard the tires on the gravel, signifying any car's approach, like at Tilly's house, but here at the ranch, three kids and three adults chatting and laughing and talking over each other—okay, that was mostly the kids—and the only signal of a visitor was the doorbell.

"I'll get it," Kel said, jumping up. "Melissa is probably trying to make sure she gets her dish back." She bent to kiss the top of Jax's head.

"You're just trying to get out of dishes," Justin teased.

"Cook doesn't clean," she sing-sang as she left the room.

Since Rex was done, he picked up his plate and stood, then gathered some of the carnage from the table and carried it all over to the sink. He'd just started the water when Justin came over.

"What are you doing to that poor girl, bro?"

Rex froze, the ice down his spine colder than the water on his hands. "I like her, Jus," he said, not willing to admit to his brother that he loved Tilly. That was for her ears only, at least the first time he said it.

After that, he could write it in the sky or buy a billboard, but the first time should be special.

Roses—no, sunflowers. Romantic words. Candles—

The thought made him smile.

Justin's sigh didn't.

"She's not for you," Justin said. "You know that. She's . . . fragile, and you'll destroy her."

"Tilly's the strongest person I know."

That sigh again, followed by a tone he knew too well. Disappointment. "Rex."

"What? You think I'm going to break her? Destroy her? You think I'm that much of an asshole?" His brother's hesitation in answering had Rex's gut sinking. "You do. You think I'm the same prick who took advantage of Kelly."

"You don't think of anyone but yourself," Justin said. "That's not your way, bro, and now Tilly is caught in the crosshairs."

"But I'm not the same."

"Who are you trying to convince?" It was a reasonable question considering his past, considering the weak ass declaration Rex had just given.

He tried again.

"I'm not that man," he said. "Not anymore. I've changed."

Justin crossed his arms, eyes not hard exactly, but something inside of them had shifted. He didn't believe Rex had changed, and he probably never would. This was all just a fucking waste of his time. He'd never find his place in this family again. Hell, he wasn't even convinced that he actually *did* deserve a spot. He'd pissed on that honor plenty of times in the past.

"What are you doing here?" Justin asked before his voice softened. "What did you expect to find?"

"Not to fall in love," he snapped. He sure as shit hadn't anticipated that curve ball.

Justin's eyes widened. "Did you say—?"

"No."

But it wasn't in response to his brother.

Tilly stood in the doorway.

Horror coursed through him. She'd heard him say he loved her, and he hadn't made it special. Fuck. She deserved special.

"I'm sorry," he began, walking toward her.

"No." She put up a hand, and he stopped.

"That's twice you said that," he murmured. "No, what?" To the apology? To the sentiment itself? To him?

"You can't mean it," she said, face pale and eyes glittering with tears. "I thought we were . . . different. You made me hope —" She choked on a sob.

"I'm sorry," he said again, pulling her into her arms. "I didn't mean for you to overhear that. I was going to tell you another way."

Her spine went ramrod stiff, and she shoved him hard enough that he stumbled back a step. "Of course, you were."

"Tilly—"

She scooted away, backing toward the door. "J-just stay away from me, Rex Roosevelt. Stay the *fuck* away."

Familiar ice coated his spine, numbed him from the inside

out. Nothing. He was better off if he felt nothing. *Wrong. This is wrong to stay away.* But before he could grasp fully on to the thought, Tilly was gone, and he was standing in the kitchen with his brother's family staring at him incredulously.

Kel and Justin both spoke at once.

It was Justin's words that struck home.

"See?" he said. "Tilly doesn't want this."

Rex was too gutted to see Kelly smack him, to watch her rise on tiptoe and whisper in his brother's ear. Too devastated to see Justin's face pale.

He left.

It was better that way.

For everyone.

TWENTY

Tilly

THE LETTER WAS under her mat the next morning.

I'm sorry you feel that way. I'd bought this for you ~~before you changed your~~ before things between us changed. Don't say no until you go and see it.

-R

Below that was an address.

"Shit," she muttered, recognizing it.

Absolutely no way was she going there, even if it was just down the street from Henry's Diner. With the way things were going, it was probably an empty room full of the candles she'd made.

Sighing, she pushed through into the diner, only to stop short.

Henry was at the hostess stand, arms crossed. "What are you doing here, Tilly?"

Her stomach clenched. "What do you mean?"

"I mean, you're not on shift today," he said, dropping his arms to rearrange the stack of menus behind the stand.

"Oh, yeah," she said, remembering he'd given her the morning off after she'd worked late the previous night. Before she'd finished up a few minutes early and had headed to the ranch to surprise Rex. Before she'd had her heart broken again because she was an idiot who'd fallen for the wrong person hook, line, and sinker. "I figured I'd come anyway. I could use the—"

She stopped herself from finishing that sentence because she didn't really need the money anymore. The shop had given her a cushion. She'd be able to pay off the outstanding bills and could easily live on her waitressing salary without the added pressure of the medical debts.

Thanks to Rex.

Her eyes burned.

"I'm sure Bella can use prep help."

Henry shook his head. "No, kiddo," he said softly. "You've been working too hard for too long. I missed it before, but you need some time off to reset."

"I'm not a kid," she muttered.

He touched her arm. "I know that's not fair to think of you that way after everything you've been through, but you've been through so much. Plus, now you've got Rex, and it's new and fresh and you seem happy with him." A nudge toward the door. "You should go enjoy yourself." A beat. "With him."

And her heart shattered a little more.

Tilly knew she was moments away from bursting into tears and so she kept her gaze down, nodded, and slipped outside the door, but when she made it to her car, it wouldn't start.

"Perfect," she said, losing her battle with the tears. They streamed down her cheeks, dripped off her jaw, turning the gray of her seat black.

She tried the key again and nothing.

"Fuck!" she said, suddenly so damned furious and upset and . . . hurt.

Alone again, heart shredded.

P.A.T.H.E.T.I.C.

She was absolutely—

No.

Not anymore. Not again. She wasn't weak or fragile or freaking pathetic. Maybe she'd been deceived and naïve, falling for the wrong man in too short of a time, but also . . . maybe she didn't have to let this destroy her.

She pulled the handle to pop the hood, then slipped from her car and spent a few minutes staring at the respective parts.

But she hadn't seen what Rex had done to get it started and so she had to resort to calling Dale. He answered on the first ring and promised to come check it out after he got his morning appointments checked in and underway.

Until then, she would wait.

Fifteen minutes later, she was going stir crazy.

She was up to date on all her shows, none of her favorite YouTubers had released videos, and was out of energy in the one game she played on her phone. And Rex's note kept staring at her from the passenger's seat.

Should she just go and see?

If it *was* candles, it would serve him right if she resold them.

Maybe she should—

"No, you will not, Tilly Conner," she told herself firmly. "Absolutely not.

But when another half hour passed and Dale still hadn't come, she found herself getting out of the car to "stretch her legs." Or at least that was the convenient lie she told herself. Couldn't let those quads tighten up, might get sore and not be able to—

She cut the lie off there and walked down to the end of the block.

To the address on the note.

Brown paper covered the windows, and she sighed at finding the For Rent sign gone. It wasn't a surprise that someone had rented the space. Darlington's downtown was a popular destination for both locals and tourists alike, so empty store-fronts didn't stay empty for long.

Tilly had just been eyeing this one because it was perfect. It had been a coffee shop and bookstore before, the walls lined with gorgeous oak shelves, the old worn tables left behind. She'd been able to picture her products on those shelves, candles on one wall, toiletries on other, maybe even makeup or a hairstylist who could come in on special days and give customers a new look—

Sigh.

It wasn't to be.

She'd keep inching her way into success. She'd keep wait-ressing and working her Etsy shop and craft fairs and—

One day everything would be fine.

See? She could be heartbroken and healthy.

Tilly walked past the front doors and rounded the building. Rex had said he was in the apartment above the store, and she thought the entrance was along the alleyway. It took a couple of tries to find the right door, but eventually she found one that was unlocked—well, slightly propped open with a thin sliver of wood. She pulled it wide, saw a flight of stairs leading up, and with a deep, bracing breath, walked up to the second floor.

The first thing that hit her was the smell.

Oh fuck, the smell. *His* smell was everywhere.

Almost a physical sensation, it crawled up her nose, coated her skin, and her eyes prickled all over again. God, how could she have been stupid enough to fall for him?

To fall in love with him.

Sighing, she stepped further into the apartment, taking in the simple studio that was so different from the house on the ranch. A table was propped in one corner, an L-shaped kitchenette surrounding it. The couch was a pale blue, the curtains a soft gray, the bed stripped of its linens, which were folded neatly at the foot of the mattress.

That neat stack of cotton did her in.

Or maybe everything that had happened did her in.

Hearing Justin warn Rex about her was bad enough. Despite everything she'd been through, everyone still thought she was weak. But worse was hearing Rex say he didn't love her, implying he never would, and the regret on his face when he'd realized she was there had burned like hell, only made worse by the half-hearted apology.

As if he thought they'd just keep going when there was no future.

It was just . . . she didn't get it.

She didn't *expect* him to love her, no matter that she'd fallen hard. It was too much too soon. But Tilly *had* expected him to be honest with her, especially after they'd shared so much of their pasts. Rex knew more about her than probably any other person on the planet and . . .

He'd thrown that away.

Which made this whole situation worse. She'd allowed herself to be vulnerable and—

Never mind. She'd forget him and move on . . .

As soon as she sorted out this wild goose chase of coming to the apartment. It wasn't like she needed to live here. This wasn't any nicer than her house, and it wasn't filled with her products from what she could see, as she'd half expected.

Sighing, she sank down onto the couch.

Maybe she should just sell her house and move. There

wasn't really anything here, and it was something she'd considered more than once in the past. She'd never had the courage to pull that particular plug before, but maybe this experience with Rex would change that because the idea of facing the town, of seeing Kelly or Henry or Justin look at her with that sad, pitying look she'd seen on Kelly's face the night before . . .

No. She couldn't live like that.

"Okay," she muttered. "Nothing here. Just another mistake when it comes to Rex Roos—*oh*." Tilly had placed her hand on the cushion next to her to push herself up to her feet, but instead of fabric, she felt paper. Or rather, a manila envelope with her name on the front.

Carefully, she opened the flap and pulled out the sheet inside.

"What?" A key was taped onto the single white piece of paper.

Not here. Downstairs.

-R

Heart pounding, she tugged the key free and before she could overthink it, Tilly pounded down the stairs and out into the alley. There was a locked door right next to the one she just exited. She'd tried it earlier, and though it hadn't budged, she thought maybe this key might work in the lock.

Her fingers shook as she inserted the key, then shook some more when it turned.

"Oh," she murmured, finding it opened to reveal a dim hallway, and she couldn't be sure if she was disappointed to see it was empty or excited that there seemed to be a light on at the end of it. "Hello?" she called, and when no one answered, she felt along the wall for a light switch and flicked it on.

Empty, except for a few items that must have belonged to the coffee shop when Carol had retired to Florida—a tray of ceramic mugs and some cleaning supplies were on the shelf, a mop bucket pushed into one corner.

"Hello?" she called again.

Nothing.

Quiet feet led her fully inside and down the hall, drawing her toward that single light like a moth to a flame . . . or an addict to Rex's scent.

Because she could smell it all around her, and it made her heart ache.

Ignoring her sudden urge to cry, knowing this was a grief that she'd get over given enough time, she kept walking until she reached the front of the store. Then gasped.

The space was the same and yet different.

The shelves had been sanded and prepped for fresh stain, same as the tables. The cooking equipment had been stacked on one side to be cataloged. A trash can, a broom, and a dustpan were in another corner.

And she was focusing on the mundane because she was deliberately avoiding the sight directly in front of her. It was so fucking heartbreakingly perfect that it threatened to take her breath away.

Artfully arranged, better than she could have imagined were her products.

Shampoo and conditioner, face masks and lip balms. Every single item she made was on that table.

Including a cinnamon roll candle.

Sitting on top of another manila envelope.

This time she knew what was inside before she opened the flap, which was a good thing because her vision was so blurry with tears that it was hard to actually read the paper, to see her name on the deed, to see mock-ups of a sign for the storefront— an exact match to her *Tilly's Treasures* logo online.

"Oh, Rex," she said, sniffing as she clutched the sheet to her chest. "How can you be so fucking perfect and leave me so easily?"

"Actually, I found I couldn't leave you."

Gasping, she whirled around, saw that Rex was in the hall. "I thought you'd gone."

His expression was careful. "I did go. Got all the way to the airport but found I couldn't leave. Not without fighting for you, for us. And so, I came back." He stepped toward her, paused with too many feet between them. "I know you don't love me, that it's too soon, because even though I'm in it deep for you, I get that you need time to trust the men in your life and—" He sucked in a breath, came close enough for her to feel his heat. "I just know that I can't just leave the woman I love without trying one more time."

Her throat was dry, her pulse pounding. "I don't understand," she said. "You told Justin you could never love me."

"I said I never expected to fall in love, sweetheart. But then there you were, a perfect angel on the side of the road, knocking me off my axis, making me realize that life is too fucking short to not go after the love of your life." He lifted his palm, hesitated with it an inch above her cheek. "That's you, by the way."

She laughed, and it was watery. "I—uh . . ." She shook her head, trying desperately to clear it. "I don't understand what's happening. You don't want to break up with me? You love me? You're not leaving?"

"God, no. Fuck yes. And hell no."

Tilly dropped her head in her hands. "So—I—"

She burst into tears and perfect man that he was, Rex tugged her close and gave her the words she needed, telling her all the parts of the conversation she'd missed, how he'd been so upset by her words and leaving that he'd decided to move on. But Kelly and Justin hadn't let him go. They'd caught him at the airport, and Kelly had kicked both of their asses on the way home—Justin for being a judging meddling fool who didn't realize that Rex had changed, and Rex for not immediately going after Tilly.

"I didn't realize you hadn't heard it all," he whispered. "Not until Kelly told me what she'd overheard, and I finally clued in to what you thought. I was such a fucking idiot for not chasing you down straight away, but my feelings were hurt, and I was running stupid, and—" He sucked in a breath. "I left you, sweetheart. I'm so damn sorry for that, most of all."

She stuck her face into the crook of his neck and inhaled, letting the scent center her for a moment. "Thank you," she murmured. "For coming back. I should have fought for us, too. I shouldn't have run off. Not when you're so damned important to me."

"It was my—"

"Let's play who was the bigger idiot later," she said, hugging him tightly. "I love you, Rex, you imperfect man. I love you because you're perfect for me. Because you're kind and thoughtful and—"

He kissed her, fierce and sweet at the same time, his tongue stroking along hers, his body hard where she was soft, and that fucking delicious *eau de* Rex making her head spin. Or maybe the lack of oxygen. Or, more likely, it was just Rex because he was loving and considerate, funny, and strong. The only person in all the world who seemed to understand what was going on in her brain and what she needed.

She'd meant what she said.

Neither of them was perfect, but he was absolutely perfect for her.

"I love you," he said, pulling back and crushing her to his chest. He held her tight for a long moment, but when he set her away from him then laced his fingers through hers and said,

"Come on. Let me show you around your shop," Tilly stopped him.

"I'd rather you show me the tabletops," she said slyly.

His brows drew together. "What?" he asked. "I sanded them down, so they'd be ready for whatever finish you wanted. Did I ruin—?"

She tore her T-shirt over her head, dropped it to the dusty floor. Then stepped out of her sneakers, shoved her jeans off, and hopped up on a table.

"Careful of splinters—" he started to warn as she jumped up, but the rest of his words never emerged because her bra joined the rest of her clothes. She crooked a finger in his direction.

"Forget the splinters," she said. "Just come over here and love me, Roosevelt."

His mouth curved into a sinful smile. "Now *that* I can do."

EPILOGUE

Rex

Four years later

REX STOOD in the doorway of Tilly's shop, cradling their nine-month-old son in his arms. Justin and Jax were having a serious conversation in one corner, while Jesse, her eyes reddened from crying, was getting a hug from Tilly.

Abigail, looking so damn grown-up, was sweeping the remnants of a broken candle from the floor, carefully carrying the full dustpan to the garbage can behind the counter.

"I'm so sorry, Aunt Tilly," Jesse was saying. "I got so mad at Jax, and I shouldn't have pushed him." She hung her head, cheeks glistening with tears.

"Come here, kiddo," Tilly said and hugged her tight. "Thank you for owning up to your mistake. That makes much more of a difference to me than one candle."

Jesse's arms were around Tilly's neck. "But the candles cost money."

His beautiful wife met his stare over Jesse's shoulder. "They do, but I know how you can pay for it."

Jesse nodded and stepped back. "I'll go home and get my piggy bank."

"No, kiddo. I want you to help me break down the boxes in the storeroom. My hands get so tired and I can't fit them in the recycle bin by myself."

"I can do that."

"I'll show you what to do."

Rex trailed Tilly, watching her explain the task to the little girl who'd just started first grade. Not even seven and yet so mature for her age already, so self-sufficient, smart, and capable—like her mama and aunties. She had great role models.

Once Jesse got going on the boxes, Tilly came over to him and hugged him tight. "How are my two favorite boys?"

"Missing you," he said softly, handing over Jordan—because his brother didn't get the copyright on J names in the Roosevelt household, and his son was as crazy about his wife as Kel and Justin's kids were. It was probably why the twins had gotten into a rare disagreement, they tended to get very competitive over their Aunt Tilly.

"It's been a busy time," she said. "I'm sorry I've been working so much."

He tugged her ponytail and went over to help Jesse with a box that was as big as her. "That's what happens when your store is so successful that you need to open up three more locations."

Tilly blushed, and it was as cute now as it had been from the first moment he'd seen her. "I love you," she murmured.

"Meh," he teased and folded the box for Jesse.

"Thanks, Uncle Rex," she said, wrestling it out the back door.

"Should I—?" He started to follow her, but Tilly stopped him.

"She's fine." A cheeky grin. "You forgot to kiss me hello."

"Hmm," he said, tapping his chin. "Do parents do that? Especially very successful, very busy, fairly new parents?"

"Shut up and get your mouth on mine."

He did as commanded, and as things were often the case now that he and Tilly had found their happy, now that they had crept in from the outside and firmly planted themselves into the center of their family, his kiss didn't go as planned.

Right when things began to heat up in all the right ways, he heard,

"Ew, Uncle Rex."

"Yes, ew!"

Jesse and Jax seemed to have finally found their common ground, and that was in the form of ew-ness. Ew-nity, one might say.

Fine. He *did* say, which garnered him an eye roll from his wife, a snort from Justin, fresh "ew"s from the twins, and giggles from Abigail. Then, fresh from the ranch, Kelly joined them, her pregnant belly leading the way, because she and his brother was expecting *another* set of twins. The chaos of the kiddos' greetings for their mother woke up Jordan, who began crying in earnest while Tilly walked and bounced him through the store.

It was insanity.

It was loud and decidedly *not* peaceful.

It was everything he could have ever dreamed of.

Rex crossed to his wife and kissed her soundly on the lips, scooping up Jordan and making silly faces at him until he settled down and demanded to be put down so he could join his cousins.

They watched Justin's brood encourage Jordan until he

managed to crawl close enough that Abigail took pity on him and carried him the last bit of the distance.

"I can't wait to make another one of those with you," he murmured.

Tilly's eyes softened. "Funny you should say that," she said, lacing their fingers together. "We might not have had much time for kissing but . . ." She brought his palm to her belly.

Holy shit.

"You're—?"

She nodded, smile huge, and he bravely risked more "ew"s because the most important thing in the world in that moment was kissing his beautiful, incredible wife.

"I fucking love you," he said when they finally had to stop for air.

Her cheeks were pink, her lips swollen, and she glanced around the shop that had gotten suspiciously quiet.

"I think Justin took a hint," she said with a laugh.

"About time," he said, laughing along with her. "Should we go rescue them?"

"Probably." Her mouth curved, her eyes mischievous. "But kiss me once more before we go."

Not one to deny his wife anything, Rex obliged.

And then kept kissing her until the "ew"s returned.

ROOSEVELT RANCH SERIES

Disaster at Roosevelt Ranch

Heartbreak at Roosevelt Ranch

Collision at Roosevelt Ranch

Regret at Roosevelt Ranch

Desire at Roosevelt Ranch

Did you miss any of the other Roosevelt Ranch books? Check out excerpts from the series below or find the full series here:
amazon.com/gp/product/B07Q8VRK9Y

DISASTER AT ROOSEVELT RANCH
Book One
(books2read.com/DARR)

USING MY BACK, I pushed through the swinging door and promptly stumbled to a stop.

He was here. *Rex* was here.

Stupidly, my heart raced. He'd changed his mind. He'd—

The man's eyes flicked to mine, completely unrecognizing and indifferent. My momentary burst of hope disintegrated.

He was going to pretend not to know me? To not *recognize* me?

The jerk! The rotten—

Except . . . there was something off about him. I squinted, trying to discern the change, but the tray was taking its toll on my arms. I tore my gaze away from Rex to practically hurl the dishes at my customers.

"Anything else?" I asked, and was thankful when there weren't any requests.

Two seconds later, I was in front of Rex.

Who wasn't *actually* Rex.

Oh, he was the right height and had the same square jaw and the same gorgeous, sun-kissed skin, but *this* man wasn't the one I'd slept with.

"Hi," he said, his green eyes warm. They were a brilliant emerald and just as inviting as they'd been in the picture I'd seen on Rex's desk. "Can I just sit anywhere?"

My nod was jerky. "I'll get you a menu."

Fingers brushed my arm—calloused fingers that felt both familiar and different.

"You okay?"

I forced a smile, my stomach churning. This could *not* be happening. "Just perfect—"

And that was the moment I puked all over Rex's twin's shoes.

—Get your copy books2read.com/DARR.

HEARTBREAK AT ROOSEVELT RANCH
Book Two
(books2read.com/HARR)

I NAVIGATED the minefield of toys as I made my way over to Max. I gave an internal grunt as I lifted the little—or not so little, anymore—monkey and tucked him back into bed.

One hastily constructed barrier of pillows and blankets and stuffed Minecraft toys later, and I was heading back out of the room.

I flicked the light off, started to leave—

"Too dark, Mommy," he murmured.

A sigh. Back on it went. "Good night, sweetheart."

"Night."

This time I made it to the top of the stairs before a sound stopped me.

It wasn't the kids. No. This was more like . . . buzzing?

I cocked my head and listened, then made my way to my bedroom, a growing pile of toys in my arms as I went.

The door was open, and I walked inside, dumping the pile on the coverlet before stopping to pinpoint the sound.

I felt my pockets for my cell. Not even two days before, I'd scoured the house for my phone, it somehow having fallen out of my pocket, ending up under the dresser. It had taken darn near fifty calls and a search of the entire house before I'd found it.

Those locating apps were all well and good, but they couldn't tell a person which room in a house their phone was. Which meant the app, for my day-to-day exploits, was pretty much useless.

I hardly left home at all except for the kids' activities and school pickup or drop off.

Or if Rob needed something down at the station.

And that was fine. My place was at home. The kids needed me, Rob needed me. It was just that sometimes . . .

No. Don't get sidetracked.

My phone *was* in my pocket. The sound wasn't coming from beneath the dresser.

It was coming from the bed.

I peered under, saw nothing, and I was reaching for Rob's

flashlight in his nightstand when I realized where exactly the noise was originating from.

My hand slid between the mattress and box spring, jumping a little when the object buzzed against my fingers.

"What—?" I pulled it out, saw it was an older-looking iPhone. Why was there—

Then I saw the texts. An entire screen worth of them.

And my heart froze solid.

I'm heading to the hotel.

Where are you?

Don't keep me waiting, honey.

I need you.

The question wasn't why Rob had hidden a phone under his side of the mattress. It was why someone named Celeste was calling him honey and telling *my* husband that she needed him.

Downstairs, I heard the garage door rumble open and close, the clink of Rob's keys on the kitchen counter. "Miss?" he called softly up the stairs.

My voice was gone, my throat tight. My eyes burned, and still, I held the phone. It wasn't until I heard him walking down the hall to the bedroom that I sprang into motion.

I shoved the phone back under the mattress and scooped up the toys.

Rob stopped short in the doorway. "Oh." He smiled. "I called you."

"Sorry, I was cleaning."

He touched my cheek, slid past me. "You don't have to do that."

"It's my job," I said brightly, and if it was too bright then what did it matter anyway?

My husband was moving toward the bathroom, already unbuttoning his shirt. "Is there a plate for me?"

I turned, saw he'd paused, and forced a smile. "Yup. I'll heat it up for you."

"Thanks, love."

"Of course." I walked out of the bedroom but didn't go downstairs.

Instead, I hesitated in the hall, silent and waiting.

And my gut tied itself into knots when I heard Rob's footfalls across the carpet, the slide of his hand beneath the mattress as he pulled out the phone.

—Get your copy at books2read.com/HARR.

COLLISION AT ROOSEVELT RANCH
Book Three
(books2read.com/CARR)

Haley

"Just play already," Haley muttered, fumbling with her phone. She'd stopped at an intersection on her way home from the hospital, and she just wanted to boy band love, okay?

Exhaustion tugged at her brain, her eyes burned, and her shoulders ached. She was also very close to tears.

She'd lost a patient that night.

It hadn't been her fault. It hadn't been anyone's fault. Sometimes those things just happened—accidents, everyone working frantically to pull someone back from the brink, a body failing— but that didn't make losing a patient any easier.

Her job was to save them.

Life was such a fragile thing. As a nurse, she knew that first-hand. But she'd also left her job at the busy county hospital in California and returned home to Darlington, Utah because she was tired of seeing people die every day.

Haley was damned good at compartmentalizing, but sometimes things weren't so easy to shove down.

Sometimes those fuckers kept popping back up.

Sometimes the cases hit too close to home—

A horn beeped behind her and she jumped. "Shit." Her phone still not cooperating, the poppy upbeat notes of her favorite boy bands remained silently trapped inside the technological device that never seemed to work correctly.

Even though it was brand spanking new.

Even though she'd gotten a complete tutorial from her brother-in-law, who had gone through all the troubleshooting with her.

Even though the freaking tech from the phone store had personally tested the Bluetooth by coming out to her car and showing her how it worked.

Technology. She repelled it.

Or rather, she was technology's kryptonite.

Two minutes around her, and she destroyed even the most powerful device.

"Yay me," she murmured, dropping the phone to her passenger's seat. Haley shouldn't be fussing with it anyway, not while she was driving, but—*a sigh*—she'd really wanted to escape for the rest of her drive.

Not to be.

Checking for traffic, she pulled carefully through the intersection. Darlington was a small town, and signals were few and far between, but the roads at this time of the night were dark . . . and she'd had a deer jump right in front of her car once before.

The car that had honked at her turned to follow her down the bumpy lane, headlights very bright in her rearview mirror, the front bumper just inside that bubble all drivers had.

This one triggered her slightly-too-close alert but not the this-fucker-better-back-off alarm.

Her lips curved.

So, she might have gotten used to the more aggressive drivers of Northern California.

The thought of her first months in San Francisco, of the busy roads, the huge buildings, the patient care that both challenged and devastated her, brought a smile to her face. For all the reasons she'd come home, Haley was still happy she'd left Utah.

Small town life was . . . well, small.

Or it had seemed that way before she'd left.

Now she saw how much her world had expanded by being . . . well, herself. Having *found* herself, as cliché as that sounded.

She'd left a little girl, never feeling like she could measure up, and had returned—

Still feeling like she would never live up to her expectations. *Ha.* That was life for a girl. But Haley had come back with the understanding that *she* was the one setting impossible standards. Progress, yes? And she was a work in progress.

Step one was realizing that not everything she did had to be perfect and exacting.

Which was all well and good for her Pinterest attempts —*cough*—fails.

It didn't work as well for her patients.

Hence the mental punch fest happening in her brain alongside the driving need for cheesy pop music to provide her with some escapism.

Had she done everything right? What had she missed?

What could she have done differently? Would any of it had made any difference?

No.

No, it wouldn't have.

Tears stung her eyes, and she blinked them away.

If Haley hadn't blinked at that moment, things might not have turned out as they did.

But she *did* blink, right as two other things happened simultaneously.

Music exploded through her speakers—the Backstreet Boys singing about the way they wanted it—and a deer jumped into the road.

By the time her lids had flashed back open, the jar of poptastic noise accelerating the process to near inhuman speed, the flipping deer was directly in front of her bumper and *definitely* within her bubble.

Frankly, it was firmly in the she-was-gonna-plow-it-down-and-make-a-deer-pancake zone.

"Fuck!" She slammed on her brakes.

Tires screeched. She braced for impact and then . . .

The deer executed a leap that was fitting of a figure skater and jumped clear of her car.

Haley sighed in relief. For a single heartbeat.

Because that relief disappeared before the next.

Her body was propelled forward as the driver who had been —and here came that damned bubble analogy again—following her too closely before, plowed into her from behind.

And she didn't even have time to snort about the dirtiness of that particular innuendo before the seatbelt yanked tightly across her chest. Pain shot up her leg as her foot compressed more firmly on the brake pedal, but before she could focus too much on the sensation, her head smacked against the top of the steering wheel.

"Fucking bubbles," she slurred as everything went black.

—Get your copy at books2read.com/CARR

REGRET AT ROOSEVELT RANCH
Book Four
(books2read.com/RARR)

Henry

Henry wiped down the final table. He was beyond ready to go home and crash after a busy Sunday evening cooking at the diner.

He'd already flicked off the neon "Open" sign and dimmed the lights. The kitchen had been scrubbed and reset for the next morning's breakfast rush, and he'd sent Tilly off about an hour earlier—she'd had a date, and Henry didn't mind sweeping up or stocking the tables with all the necessities for the next day.

Paper napkins, ketchup, salt and pepper, sugar. They weren't what had been on the tables in the Michelin-starred restaurant he'd cooked at while living in New York five years before, but they were his childhood.

His way of feeling close to his dad.

God, he missed his dad.

The bell hanging on the front door rang, and he mentally cursed at having forgotten to lock it.

Beginner mistake.

He'd worked half his childhood in the diner, had closed it down more times than he could count.

And somehow, he'd forgotten to lock the front door.

Hopeless.

"I'm sorry, we're closed," he said, deliberately not looking as he reached to straighten a salt shaker that was slightly askew.

"So, this is your place, is it?" The softly accented voice made him freeze.

Italy. Warm Tuscan sunlight, softly rolling hills through wine country. Cheese and pasta and pizza and . . . *her*.

He accidentally knocked the shaker to the floor. It didn't break because this was a family place and they'd learned long ago that plastic was safer with the kiddos, but Henry watched in slow horror as the lid popped off and salt spread out on the tile floor.

Though his horror didn't come from the spilled salt.

No. It came from the fact that she was there.

He turned. Saw for sure he hadn't been mistaken.

She was there.

Isabella Mariano was in Darlington, Utah. Inside his restaurant.

"*Buona notte*, Henry."

He'd last seen her as she'd gotten on a plane heading the opposite direction of where he'd needed her, flying away when he'd asked her to stay, bolting while his heart had been left to shatter.

"Isabella," he said coldly.

If she noticed his tone, she didn't comment on it.

Then again, she was good at that.

"What are you doing here?" he prompted when she didn't say anything further.

She swept over to him, heels clicking on the tile floor, more beautiful than ever. Her brown hair fell in perfect waves, her killer body was clad in sleek designer clothes, and a diamond ring on her left ring finger sparkled in the dim light.

Diamond ring.

On her left hand.

He processed that, but her words still hit him like a two-by-four to the temple.

"I want you to cater my wedding."

—Get your copy at books2read.com/RARR

ALSO BY ELISE FABER

Roosevelt Ranch Series (all stand alone)

Disaster at Roosevelt Ranch

Heartbreak at Roosevelt Ranch

Collision at Roosevelt Ranch

Regret at Roosevelt Ranch

Desire at Roosevelt Ranch (November 17th)

Billionaire's Club (all stand alone)

Bad Night Stand

Bad Breakup

Bad Husband

Bad Hookup

Bad Divorce

Bad Boyfriend (Oct 6th, 2019)

Gold Hockey (all stand alone)

Blocked

Backhand

Boarding

Benched

Breakaway

Breakout (Dec 15th, 2019)

Life Sucks Series (all stand alone)

Train Wreck

Phoenix Series (series, rereleasing October 21st)

Phoenix Rising

Dark Phoenix

Phoenix Freed

Phoenix: LexTal Chronicles (rereleasing soon, stand alone, Phoenix world)

From Ashes

KTS Series

Fire and Ice (Hurt Anthology, stand alone)

ABOUT THE AUTHOR

USA Today bestselling author, Elise Faber, loves chocolate, Star Wars, Harry Potter, and hockey (the order depending on the day and how well her team -- the Sharks! -- are playing). She and her husband also play as much hockey as they can squeeze into their schedules, so much so that their typical date night is spent on the ice. Elise is the mom to two exuberant boys and lives in Northern California. Connect with her in her Facebook group, the Fabinators or find more information about her books at www.elisefaber.com.

f facebook.com/elisefaberauthor

a amazon.com/author/elisefaber

BB bookbub.com/profile/elise-faber

O instagram.com/elisefaber

g goodreads.com/elisefaber

P pinterest.com/elisefaberwrite